Wedding Song

The following titles by Naguib Mahfouz
are also published by Doubleday
and Anchor Books:

THE THIEF AND THE DOGS
THE BEGINNING AND THE END

NAGUIB MAHFOUZ

Wedding Song

Translated from Arabic by
Olive E. Kenny
Edited and revised by
Mursi Saad El Din and
John Rodenbeck
Introduction by
Mursi Saad El Din

Doubleday
New York London Toronto Sydney Auckland

PUBLISHED BY DOUBLEDAY

A division of Bantam Doubleday Dell Publishing Group, Inc.
666 Fifth Avenue, New York, New York 10103

DOUBLEDAY and the portrayal of an anchor with a dolphin
are trademarks of Doubleday, a division of Bantam Doubleday
Dell Publishing Group, Inc.

This English translation was first published by
The American University in Cairo Press in 1984.
First published in Arabic as *Afrah al-Qubbah* in 1981.
Protected under the Berne Convention.
The Doubleday edition is published by arrangement
with The American University in Cairo Press.

Library of Congress Cataloging-in-Publication Data
Maḥfūẓ, Najīb, 1911–
    [Afrāḥ al-qubbah.   English]
    Wedding song / Naguib Mahfouz; translated
    from Arabic by Olive E. Kenny; edited and
    revised by Mursi Saad El Din and John
    Rodenbeck; introduction by Mursi Saad El Din.
    1st Doubleday ed.
        p.   cm.
    Translation of: Afrāḥ al-qubbah.
    I. Saad El Din, Mursi.   II. Rodenbeck, John.
III. Title.
[PJ7846.A46A6913   1989]   89-7893
892'.736—dc20   CIP

ISBN 0-385-26463-1   ISBN 0-385-26464-X (pbk.)
Copyright © 1984 by The American University in Cairo Press
ALL RIGHTS RESERVED
PRINTED IN THE UNITED STATES OF AMERICA
FIRST DOUBLEDAY EDITION: 1989

DC

CONTENTS

FOREWORD

The English title *Wedding Song* is an attempt to preserve some of the multiple ironies in the Arabic title *Afrah al-Qubbah*. Literally, *Afrah al-Qubbah* might be interpreted as meaning something like "wedding festivities at the saint's tomb." This is a Cairene tale, however, and in this instance *al-qubbah* refers to a palace that was one of the official residences of the former khedives of Egypt. Naguib Mahfouz explained to me that the weddings of the khedivial family were marked by processions with singing and dancing, and that songs sung on these occasions, popularly repeated, came to be known as *afrah al-qubbah*. Hence *Wedding Song*.

O.E.K.

INTRODUCTION

Naguib Mahfouz is regarded as the leading Arabic novelist and one of the few of world stature. He is therefore one of the most translated Egyptian writers, matched in this respect only by Tawfik el-Hakim. The translation of his works remains a brave venture, however, not just because Arabic in general abounds with nuances but also because Mahfouz in particular has a style that poses a special challenge to translators, however accomplished they might be.

Afrah al-Qubbah is among the latest of his books. First published in 1981, it reflects the most recent phase in the development of this remarkable writer, who has produced more than twenty-five novels and several collections of short stories. Born in 1911 in the picturesque Gamaliyya quarter of Cairo, Mahfouz pursued philosophical studies from early youth onward, obtaining his B.A. at Cairo University (then Fouad University) in 1934. An avid reader in both English and French, he translated James Baikie's *Ancient Egypt* from English while still an undergraduate. This book became the inspiration of two early historical romances, *Radobis* and *Kifah Tibu*

(The Struggle of Thebes), published in 1943 and 1944.

Between 1945 and 1957 Mahfouz published what one can describe as "realist" novels, including *Khan el-Khalili*, *Midaq Alley*, *The Mirage*, *The Beginning and the End*, and the Cairo Trilogy, for which he was awarded the State Prize for Literature in 1957. Since 1959 Mahfouz's novels have taken a different turn, making use of symbolism and allegory to achieve fresh philosophical and psychological dimensions. Critics regard much of his more recent work as experimental.

Any novelist learns from his predecessors. The novel is young in Arabic and Mahfouz has perforce absorbed the work of many non-Arab writers. Chief among them, according to his own testimony, are Flaubert, Balzac, Zola, Camus, Tolstoy, and Dostoyevsky, all of whom he has read in French. Perhaps the most important Western influence, however, has been that of Proust. As a university student Mahfouz made a special study of the philosophy of Henri Bergson, Proust's cousin, who had codified elements that would later become central to Proust's work; and his subsequent intensive reading of *A la Recherche du Temps Perdu* has had a lasting impact especially on his idea of time.

Time is a constant theme in all his novels and a constant preoccupation of his characters. Mahfouz' works are typically laced with sentences—such as "Time is a terrible companion," "What has time done to my friend? It has imposed a hideous mask on his face"—that suggest almost a *horror temporis*.

In this novel we are prompted to see how time works changes, transforming love into hate, beauty into ugliness, loyalty into treachery, idealism into debauchery, leaving its marks on Tariq Ramadan, Karam Younis, Halima al-Kabsh, Abbas Karam Younis, and even on the old house where Abbas grew up. Like all the novels of Mahfouz, *Wedding Song* may thus be regarded in part as a history of time and its impact on character. Avoiding such commonplace information as the age of the protagonists, Mahfouz gives us instead an evocation of what has happened to their features, their bodies, the looks in their eyes, the despair in their hearts. The techniques he favors for such evocation—stream of consciousness and interior monologue—lead to narratives in the first person. Each of his main characters thus tells his or her own story, supplies us with only a personal interpretation, creates in effect his or her own theatrical drama out of the raw materials of life. The future of each may be unknown, lost in the intricacies of present and past, which are woven by each character into a single dark strand that he or she follows alone, but even Abbas, debut even Abbas, despite his success, momentarily believes that death is, sooner or later, the only future for him, as well as for all mankind.

Ultimately, however, what interests us in *Wedding Song* is not this forbidding motif or the plight of mankind, but how four very different kinds of minds and temperaments apprehend and deal with the realities that surround them. There is reason to believe that Abbas's sense of triumph at the end of the book is by no means illusory. Unlike the other characters, he has been able to transform his own life; and he has also transformed theirs, through a creative power exercised almost unawares. It is his dawning consciousness of this power, which Mahfouz describes in the last pages of the book's final section, that provides us with a masterful portrait of the mind of an artist.

It is this portrait, which undoubtedly includes elements of Mahfouz's own vision of himself, that the translator has sought above all to liberate from the limitations imposed by barriers of culture and language.

MURSI SAAD EL DIN

Wedding Song

TARIQ RAMADAN THE ACTOR

September. The beginning of autumn. The month of preparations and rehearsals. In the stillness of the manager's office, where the closed windows and drawn curtains allow no other noise to intrude but the soft hum of the air conditioner, the voice of Salim al-Agrudy, our director, erupts, scattering words and ideas, sweeping through the scaffolding of our silent attentiveness. Before each speech his glance alerts the actor or actress who will be playing the part and then the voice goes on, sometimes soft, sometimes gruff, taking its cue from whether the part is a man's or a woman's. Images of stark reality rush forth, overwhelming us with their brutal directness, their daunting challenge.

At the head of an oblong table with a green baize top, Sirhan al-Hilaly, our producer, sits in command, following the reading with his hawklike features fixed in a poker face, staring at us while we crane in al-Agrudy's direction, his full lips clamped around a Deenwa cigar. The intensity of his concentration makes any interruption or comment impossible; the silence with which he ignores our excitement is so arctic that it compels us to repress it.

Doesn't the man understand the significance of what he's reading to us?

The scenes that unroll before my imagination are tinged with bloodshed and brutality. I'd like to start talking with someone to break the tension, but the thick cloud of smoke in the room deepens my sense of alienation; and I am sodden with some kind of fear. To hold back panic, I pin my eyes to the impressive desk in the rear of the room or a picture on the wall—Doria as Cleopatra committing suicide with the viper, Ismail as Antony orating over the body of Caesar—but my mind shows me the gallows. I feel devils inside me carousing.

Salim al-Agrudy utters the words "Final curtain," and all heads turn toward Sirhan al-Hilaly in bewilderment, as he says, "I'd like to know what you think of it."

Doria, our star, smiles and says, "Now I know why the author didn't come to the reading."

"Author?" I venture, convinced that somehow the world has come to an end. "He's nothing but a criminal. We ought to hand him over to the public prosecutor."

"Watch yourself, Tariq!" al-Hilaly barks at me. "Put everything out of your mind except the fact that you're an actor." I start to object, but he cuts me off irritably—"Not a word!"—and turns back to Salim, who murmurs, "It's an alarming play."

"What do you mean?"

"I'm wondering what kind of impact it'll have on the public."

"I have approved it and I feel confident."

"But the shock is almost too much."

Ismail, the male star of the troupe, mutters, "My role is disgusting."

"No one is crueler than an idealist," says al-Hilaly. "Who's responsible for all the carnage in this world? Idealist. Your role is tragic in the highest dimension."

"The murder of the baby," Salim al-Agrudy interjects. "It will destroy any sympathy the audience might have had for him."

"Let's not bother with details now. The baby can be left out. Not only has Abbas Younis persuaded me at last to accept a play of his, but I also have a feeling that it will be one of the biggest hits in the history of our theater."

Fuad Shalaby, the critic, says, "I share your opinion," and adds, "But we must cut out the baby."

"This is no play!" I exclaim. "It's a confession. It's the truth. We ourselves are actually the characters in it."

"So what?" al-Hilaly retorts, dismissing my objection. "Do you suppose that escaped me? I recognized you, of course, just as I recognized myself. But how is the audience going to know anything?"

"One way or another, the news will leak out."

"Let it! The one who'll suffer most is the author. For us, it can only mean success. Isn't that right, Fuad?"

"I'm sure that's true."

"It must be presented," al-Hilaly says, smiling for the first time, "with the utmost subtlety and propriety."

"Of course. That goes without saying."

"The public," Salim al-Agrudy mutters. "How will it go down with them?"

"That's my responsibility," replies al-Hilaly.

"Fine. We'll begin at once."

The meeting is over, but I stay behind to be alone with al-Hilaly. On the strength of the fact that we're old friends and comrades as well as former neighbors, I take the liberty of urging him to put the matter before the public prosecutor.

"Here's an opportunity for you," he says, ignoring my agitation, "to portray on the stage what you have actually experienced in real life."

"Abbas Younis is a criminal, not an author!"

"And it's an opportunity that could make you an important actor. You've played supporting roles for so long."

"These are *confessions*, Sirhan. How can we let the criminal get away with it?"

"It's an exciting play. It's bound to attract audiences and that's all that matters to me, Tariq."

Anger and bitterness well up inside me; past sorrows, with all their attendant regrets and failures, spread over my consciousness like a cloud. Then a thought comes to me: now I'll have a chance to get back at my old enemy. *"How do you know all this?" "Pardon me, but we're going to be married."*

"What are you going to do?" says Sirhan al-Hilaly.

"My primary concern is to see that the criminal gets what he deserves."

"Better make it your primary concern to learn your part."

I give in. "I won't let this chance slip by me."

At the sight of the coffin, a sense of defeat overwhelms me, and to everyone's astonishment, as if it were the first coffin I've ever seen, I burst into tears. It is neither grief nor contrition I suffer, but temporary insanity. The contemptuous expressions of the other mourners waver like water snakes in my tear-filled eyes, and I avoid looking at them, afraid my sobbing will turn to hysterical laughter.

What melancholy engulfs me as I plunge into the crowd—the men, women, and children, the dust and the din—at Bab al-Shariya!* I haven't gone

* A quarter in the northwest section of the old Fatimid quarter of Cairo.

near it for years, this district of piety and depravity, where everything under the clear autumn sky seems draped in contempt and depression. My memories of this place—bringing Tahiya here for the first time, her arm gaily tucked in mine—disgust and pain me, as much as the way I live now, mixing with scum, crouching under Umm Hany's wings. Damn the past and the present. Damn the theater. Damn its bit parts. Damn my hopes of success in a lead role—at my age, over fifty, in a play by my enemy, who is a criminal! I walk down the narrow serpentine length of the gravel merchants' market, past its ancient brooding gates and its two apartment buildings, stark and new, to the place where the old house, a dark and bloody past locked up inside it, still lurks.

Some changes have been made, though: the ground-floor reception room has been converted into a shop where watermelon seeds are roasted and sold, and Karam Younis sits in it ready for business, with his wife, Halima, beside him. Prison has transformed them completely. Their faces incarnate resentment and at the very time their son's star is on the rise they seem to have sunk into total despair.

The man catches sight of me, the woman looks in my direction, and their gazes are neither affectionate nor even cordial. I raise my hand in greeting to Karam, but he ignores it. "Tariq Ramadan!"

he rasps. "What brings you here?" Hardly expecting a better reception, I pay no attention to his brusqueness. She jumps to her feet, then immediately sits down again on her straw-bottomed chair. "The first visit we've had since our return to the face of the earth!" she says coldly. Her features still clutch at some memory of beauty and he seems to have his wits about him in spite of what he's been through—this pair who have engendered the criminal author.

Feeling that I should say something to soften the situation, I remark that the world is full of trouble and that I am merely one of the lost.

"You're like a nightmare," says Karam.

"I'm no worse than anyone else." Since neither invites me to sit down in the shop, I have to stand there like a customer, which makes me more determined to stick to the purpose of my visit.

"Well?" Karam barks at me.

"I have bad news."

"Bad news doesn't mean a thing to us," says Halima.

"Even if it's about Mr. Abbas Younis?"

Her eyes become apprehensive. "You'll always be his enemy," she spits at me, "right to the end!"

"He's a devoted son. When I refused to return to my old job at the theater, he set us up in this little shop."

"And his play's been accepted," Halima adds proudly.

"It was read to us yesterday."

"I am sure it's a marvelous piece of work."

"It's horrible. Do you know anything about it?"

"Nothing."

"He couldn't tell you."

"Why?"

"Why?! Because his play takes place in this house of yours! It tells exactly what went on inside. He exposes a crime. And it throws new light on everything that's happened!"

Karam is suddenly concerned. "What do you mean?" he asks.

"You'll see yourselves in it, just as the rest of us do. He shows everything. Everything! Don't you want to hear about it?"

"Even prison?"

"Even prison—and Tahiya's death. It shows who betrayed you to the police, and it shows that Tahiya didn't just die. She was murdered."

"What kind of nonsense is this?"

"It's Abbas, or the one who represents him in the play, who kills her."

"What do you mean?" Halima screeches in sudden fury. "You hate Abbas!"

"I'm one of his victims, and so are you."

"Isn't it just a play?" says Karam.

"It leaves no doubt about who squealed on you
or who the murderer is."

"Nonsense!"

"Abbas can explain everything," Halima says.

"Go see the play for yourselves."

"You crazy fool! You've been blinded by hate!"

"Not by hate. By the crime."

"You're nothing but a criminal yourself. And it's
only a play."

"It's the truth."

"You're a spiteful lunatic! My son may be stupid,
but he's neither an informer nor a murderer."

"He's an informer and a murderer, and not at all
stupid."

"That's what you want to believe."

"Tahiya's murderer must be brought to justice!"

"The same old spite. How did you treat Tahiya
when she was with you? Did you treat her right?"

"I loved her, that's enough."

"Yes, the love of a layabout."

"I'm a better man than your husband or your
son!" I shout.

"Just what do you want?" Karam growls, his
voice harsh with loathing.

"A piaster's worth of melon seeds!"

"Go to hell!"

As I wade back through a swarm of children and
women, my thoughts are fixed on the play. I am

certain that Abbas has not revealed the plot of his play to his parents, which in itself is a proof of his guilt. But why should he divulge such a dark secret when nobody dreamt of suspecting it? Yearning for success at any price? Will he be rewarded with fame, I wonder, rather than the gallows? *"Tariq! What can I say? It's fate. And luck!"* At the corner where the road meets Sharia al-Gaysh, I turn to the left in the direction of al-Ataba, walking toward the apartment building down a street that over the years has become shadowy, pockmarked, and constricted.

Tahiya, you got what was coming to you. If the man who killed you is the one you left me for, that's justice. Soon it'll be so crowded that people will start eating each other. If it weren't for Umm Hany, I'd be a derelict. The height of your glory, Abbas, will be the hangman's noose. And what about me? The only distinction I have is virility. My failure is otherwise indelible. Is there any meaning in the life of a third-rate actor?

Lust was my teacher in the good old days and it was lust that educated me in the sweet talk of a perfect man-about-town. Our affair was born backstage: I got Tahiya's first kiss while the others were onstage plotting the death of Rasputin.

"Tahiya, you deserve to be a star, not a second-rate actor like me."

"Do you really think so? You're exaggerating, Mr. Tariq."

"Not at all. It's the voice of experience."

"Or the eye of approval?"

"Even love doesn't color my judgment."

"Love!"

We'd been walking after midnight along Sharia Galal, oblivious to the biting cold, intoxicated by the warmth of our dreams. "Of course," I answered. "Shall we take this taxi?"

"It's time for me to go home."

"Alone?"

"There's no one else in my little flat."

"Where do you live?"

"Sharia al Gaysh."

"We're almost neighbors. I have a room at Bab al-Shariya, in Karam Younis's house."

"The prompter?"

"Yes. Are you going to ask me up to your flat, or shall I invite you to my place?"

"What about Karam and Halima?" I laughed, and she smiled. "There's no one else in the house?"

"They've only got one kid. He's a student." She was pretty. She had a flat. And her salary was the same as mine.

Why has Sirhan al-Hilaly sent for me in the middle of rehearsals? Leaning across the conference table in the warm sunlight, he speaks before I have a chance to say anything: "You've asked to be excused from rehearsals twice, Tariq?" I say nothing, and he goes on: "Don't mix friendship with work. Isn't it enough that you have driven Abbas into hiding?"

"Perhaps the reason he fled is that he's been exposed."

"Are you still clinging to those strange ideas of yours?"

"He's a criminal. No doubt about it."

"It's a play. And you're an actor, not a public prosecutor."

"But he's a criminal. And you know it as well as I do!"

"Your judgment is blinded by hate."

"I don't bear any grudge."

"Haven't you recovered yet from unrequited love?"

"Our rehearsing is going to bring success to a criminal!"

"It will be our success—and your chance after years of obscurity to be seen in the limelight."

"Please, Sirhan, life. . . ."

"Don't talk to me about life. Don't start philosophizing! I hear that stuff onstage every night and I'm sick of it. You've neglected your health. Sex, drugs, and the wrong kind of food. In that play about the female martyr you took the role of the

Imam* when you were drunk, without the slightest twinge of conscience."

"You're the only one who knew it."

"There was more than one member of the faithful out front who could smell your breath. Are you going to force me to. . . ."

"Don't treat the friendship of a lifetime as if it were nothing," I break in, alarmed.

"And you recited a verse from the Koran incorrectly. That's unpardonable."

"Nothing happened."

"I beg you, please. Forget this obsession of yours, this prying and spying, and concentrate on learning your part. It's the chance of a lifetime." As I leave the room he adds, "And you'd do well to treat Umm Hany better. If she leaves you, you'll really be in a bad way."

She's the same age as I am, damnit, and doesn't have the sense to feel grateful. She watched Tahiya die, and couldn't see that she'd been murdered, leaving me to play the role of the forsaken lover night after night, to cry again and again—in front of her coffin, because she died without remorse, without even thinking about me, without knowing herself that she'd been murdered, killed by that idealist who commits suicide in the play, and should be hanged in real life.

* Prayer leader in Muslim prayers.

This crime is creating an author and an actor in one stroke.

"Isn't Tahiya coming?"

"No."

"I didn't see her at the theater."

"She's not going to the theater."

"What do you mean, Abbas?"

"Mr. Tariq—excuse me—Tahiya isn't coming here and she's not going to the theater."

"How do you know all this?"

"Pardon me, but we're going to be married."

"What?!"

"We've decided to get married."

"You son of a bitch. Are you crazy? What are you saying?"

"Be reasonable. We wanted to be nice to you, to treat you with respect. Allow me...."

I slapped his face and all of a sudden he became a tiger, snarling with hatred. He punched me—a powerful young man despite his clouded left eye— and my head swam.

Karam Younis and Halima came up yelling, "What happened?"

"It's ludicrous!" I shouted. "A joke! Mama's boy is going to marry Tahiya!"

"Is that so?" said Karam in the dim voice of an addict still on a high, remote and uninvolved.

"Tahiya!" Halima exploded at her son. "What

kind of lunacy is this? She's ten years older than you?"

Abbas said nothing.

"Kids' games!" I shouted. "I'll find a way to stop this!"

"Don't make matters worse!" Halima screamed.

"I'll bring destruction on this house and everyone in it!" I shouted.

"Take your clothes," she told me coolly, "and get out."

"You can stay here and rot!" I shouted, storming out of the house.

I was shattered, though. My self-esteem went down like a stallion biting the dust. And it was just at this point, when my spirits were at rock bottom, that my heart leapt aflame with love. I'd thought my feelings were smothered in routine. I'd taken it for granted that Tahiya belonged to me, like a comfortable old shoe. I'd harangued her, demeaned her, and beaten her, but she couldn't live without me, I thought, and she'd sacrifice her life rather than leave me. Now I knew that if she walked out on me—so cunningly and so cruelly—she was taking my trust in life, my confidence, and my sense of mastery with her. What replaced them was madness—in the shape of love, which broke out of the dark corner of its lair, shook off the lethargy of long hibernation, and went to seek the food it had been missing.

When she appeared at the judas, summoned by my ringing, Tahiya's eyes showed confusion, as if she might be faltering. But they didn't flinch, there was no sign of cringing from challenge at this crisis in her life. And in what seemed a new personality, courageous, freed from continual submission, looking forward to a new life, I sensed that she was slipping across some kind of border into a region of potential violence.

"Open the door, Tahiya," I pleaded.

"You know everything now."

"Are you going to leave me outside, like a stranger?"

"Tariq, what can I say? Perhaps it's for the good of both of us. It's our fate."

"This is some crazy joke."

"I should have told you myself."

"But I don't believe it. Open up!"

"No. I'm treating you honorably."

"You're nothing but a whore!"

"Fine, then. Leave me in peace."

"I'll never do that."

"We're getting married right away."

"A student. Mad. Half blind."

"I'll try my luck."

"Open the door, you fool."

"No. It's all over between us."

"It can't be."

"That's life."

"You'll never know love except with me."

"We couldn't go on living like that."

"You're not old enough to have given up hope.
Why are you acting in this stupid fashion?"

"Please, let's be friends, I beg you."

"You acted in a fit of despair. It was a mistake."

"No."

"People like you—I know what odd phases they
go through."

"May God forgive you."

"You lunatic! When did you change?"

"I haven't committed any sin against you."

"You've lived a lie for quite some time."

"Don't keep on insisting. It's no use."

"You're the biggest whore around."

She clicked the judas shut.

For a while I actually stayed on at Karam Younis's house—Abbas Younis had left, taking over his
father's job as prompter, which the old man no
longer needed, being content with the earnings the
house made for him—and the atmosphere to begin
with was somewhat strained. Sirhan al-Hilaly took
me aside. "Don't spoil our soirees," he whispered.
"Be sensible. You can get Umm Hany back with a
wink, you know. She earns twice as much as Tahiya." Al-Hilaly is crazy about women and he'd had

Tahiya once or twice, but he knows nothing about love and can't see any connection between suffering and sex, which he ordains or disdains as if it were a matter of administrative routine. When he wants it, it's simply served up immediately. I had no doubt about his good intentions toward me: he'd given me many chances, all of which came to nothing only because of my own limitations—and now in Abbas's play he believes I'll finally be a success —so that when he told me he'd already given hints to Umm Hany about my returning to her, I went back to the company's seamstress. I did it more for the sake of escaping loneliness and shoring up the sad state of my finances than to get over any bitter emotional experience. The fact was that I expected Tahiya's marriage to fail: she'd always had attachments—she needed the money—but I was sure she'd never love anyone except me, in spite of my poverty. On the face of it she belied my expectations, keeping up her marriage until her death. The play, however, unveils her secret: she is shown confessing on her sickbed that she's sold herself to a foreigner, whereupon her husband decides to kill her by replacing her medicine with plain aspirin. So my doubts were justified without my knowing it. This man, whose idealism had been a thorn in our flesh, killed her—this man who, if it is left to me, will never escape punishment.

* * *

What have I hoped to gain? I'm face to face with Abbas in the flat that was once Tahiya's, having gone there the day after the reading, after seeing his parents in their shop. So he's now a playwright—a playwright at last, after dozens of rejections—this scribbling phony who plunders reality without shame. He's astonished to see me.

Don't be surprised, I want to tell him. What's past is past, but its aftermath, thanks to you, is going to be felt far and wide, all over again.

Al-Hilaly made peace between us one day and we've shaken hands, but we haven't buried our feelings. Here in his study—the flat consists of two rooms with a little foyer—we look at each other sullenly until I say, "No doubt you're wondering why I came."

"I trust it's good news."

"I came to congratulate you on the play."

"Thanks," he replies lukewarmly.

"Rehearsals begin tomorrow."

"Your producer is full of enthusiasm."

"Not like our director."

"What's he say?"

"The hero is a disgusting creature and the public won't like him."

He shrugs, frowning.

"Why weren't you at the reading?" I ask him.

"That's my business."

"Didn't you stop to think? What takes place in the play could create suspicion about you."

"I don't care if it does."

"They will think, quite understandably, that you're a murderer, and a traitor to your parents."

"That's ridiculous. And anyway, why should I care!"

Losing control, I blurt out, "You're a self-confessed murderer!"

"And you're nothing but a shit," he mutters, looking at me with scorn.

"Will you be able to defend yourself?"

"I haven't been accused. I don't need to defend myself."

"You'll be accused—sooner than you think."

"You're an idiot."

I get up. "She may well have deserved to be killed," I say. "But you deserve to hang."

The next day, at the first rehearsal, I'm welcomed by one of al-Hilaly's tantrums. When our producer gets angry he's a hurricane! "You! You! You're behaving like a ten-year-old!" he shouts. "An imbecile! If you weren't so stupid you could have developed into a fine actor. But you insist on turning yourself into a public prosecutor. Why did you go see Abbas Younis?" Has that bastard been complaining about me? I choose to say nothing until this storm blows over a little. "You'll never get a grip on your role," he yells, "until you concentrate on it, instead of on him."

"Today's the first day," I mumble. "It's just as important that the criminal gets what he deserves."

"There's not one of us," he bellows sarcastically, "who hasn't got some misdeed hanging around his neck for which he deserves to go to jail."

"But we haven't gone so far as to commit murder!"

"Who knows? Tahiya—if it's true that she was killed—had more than one man possibly involved in her murder. And you are chief among them."

"He doesn't deserve your defense."

"I don't consider him accused. Have you got one bit of evidence against him?"

"The play."

"No play is devoid of some charge or other. The office of the public prosecutor demands quite a different kind of evidence."

"In the play he commits suicide."

"Which means that in real life he does not commit suicide. And it's our good fortune that he'll be around to write some more."

"He never created one line, and he'll never write one. You know perfectly well what kind of plays he offered you before."

"Tariq Ramadan, don't be so tiresome! Pay attention to your work and take advantage of this opportunity, because it isn't going to come your way again."

I become absorbed in my role. Rehearsing that murderer's play, I relive my life with Tahiya, from its beginning backstage and the old house in the gravel market where we made love in my room, to the denunciation of Karam and Halima, and finally to my crying at her funeral.

"You're acting like you never acted before," Salim al-Agrudy remarks, "but you must stick to the text."

"I'm repeating what was actually said."

He laughs. "Forget about real life and live in the play!"

"You're lucky to have the right to change it."

"Just the necessary cuts. I dropped the scene about the baby."

"I have an idea!" Al-Agrudy looks annoyed, but I go on anyway: "As the heroine is dying, she asks to see her former lover."

"What lover? Every actor in this theater was her lover at one time or another."

"I mean the lover whose part I'm playing. He goes to see her, and she apologizes to him for her infidelity and dies in his arms."

"That would mean introducing major changes in their personalities and in the relationship—the bond of affection—between the husband and the wife."

"But . . ."

"You're inventing a new play. The heroine here forgets her former lover altogether."

"Impossible. And unnatural, too."

"I told you to live in the play and forget about life. Or go ahead and write a new play. There's quite a lot of sloppy, offbeat writing on the market these days."

"But you cut out the baby!"

"That's different. It has no connection with the basic plot, and the killing of an innocent baby is enough to deprive the hero of any sympathy."

"But he kills his wretched wife."

"Listen, hundreds of men in the audience wish, in their hearts, that they could kill their wives, too!"

Isn't that Karam Younis? That's him, for sure, leaving al-Hilaly's office. Only two weeks to go before the play opens. At the doorway of the cafeteria I stand chatting with Doria, the star of our company, the two of us with coffee cups in hand. As Karam approaches, dressed in his old suit, the neck of his black sweater pulled right up to his jawline, I call out, "Glad to see you here."

Casting a look at me, he growls, "Get out of my sight," nods at Doria, and goes on his way.

Doria breaks off what she was saying about the high cost of living to remark, "He must have come to ask about Abbas's mysterious disappearance."

"Abbas is hiding because he's a criminal."

"He didn't kill anyone," she assures me with a smile, "and he hasn't committed suicide."

"He may not have committed suicide. But he's certainly going to hang."

"Victory* should have led us to a more prosperous life," Doria goes on, returning to the subject at hand.

"Only the corrupt have it easy. The whole country's become one huge brothel. Why did the police bother to choose Karam Younis's house for a raid? He was only doing what everyone else does."

"We're living in times when sex has become a national pursuit," Doria says, laughing.

"I'm a man so sunk in corruption that I've been disowned by an old respectable family. So why am I still bogged down in failure?"

"The eternal failure! Poor man. No field of operation left to exploit but Umm Hany!"

On opening night, the tenth of October, the air outside is mild, but inside it feels as though it's going to be steamy. Karam and Halima, al-Hilaly, and Fuad Shalaby are among the audience. Though I'm the only one acting out on the stage what

* Refers to October 1973.

38

he experienced in reality—Ismail has the part of
Abbas—the life of the old house is lived again in
all its shamelessness with new and more brutal
crimes added. Scandals follow one after another—
the producer takes the risk of actually sneaking into
Halima's bedroom—and are crowned with betrayal
and murder. And during all this, for the first time
in my career, my acting is greeted with applause.
Is Tahiya watching us from her grave?

Pouring us out success like wine, the crowd either listens in deathly silence or bursts into wild
applause. The author, of course, criminal and cow-
ardly, is absent. But how are Karam and Halima
taking it? Before the final curtain they're going to
have a few more wrinkles in their faces.

After the show, when we have our usual celebration in the cafeteria, people, for once, seem
aware of my presence. I am altogether a different
person. From a nobody, Tahiya has made me more
than a man. The broad grin on Umm Hany's face
spreads until her mouth is as wide as a bulldog's.
Behind every great man there's a woman.

"Didn't I tell you?" says Sirhan al-Hilaly.

"A great actor has been born," adds Fuad Shalaby.

Ismail's simper shows his jealousy: it's I who've
played the complex role of a lover, a madman, and

a heel. I fill my stomach with shawerma and cognac; and the cognac reacts with the wine of success to the point where, seeing Halima in a suit she's rented from Umm Hany, I even drink a toast to the absent author.

Around three o'clock in the morning I leave the theater, arm in arm with Umm Hany and Fuad Shalaby. "Come on," says Fuad. "Let's take a stroll around Cairo at the only time it has a chance to be respectable."

"But we're a long way from home," protests Umm Hany.

"I have my car. I need to get some information."

"You're going to write about me?"

"Of course."

I crow with laughter.

Answering his questions as we walk, I tell him about my past: "I was born in Manshiyyat al-Bakri. There were two villas side by side—the Ramadan family and the al-Hilaly family. My father, Ramadan, was a major general in the cavalry, one of the pashas of the old order; al-Hilaly's was a landowner. I was the eldest in our family, and Sirhan was an only child. One of my brothers is a consul, another is a judge of the High Court, and the third is an engineer. My story in a nutshell is that we were expelled—Sirhan and I—from school. Not that we'd learned much, except about whorehouses,

taverns, and drugs. My father left me nothing. Sirhan inherited seventy feddans,* though, and to satisfy his craze for bossing and for girls, he founded
a theatrical troupe. I was one of his actors. My
brothers cut off relations with me completely. A
low salary. Debts all over the place. If it hadn't
been for women. . . ."

Umm Hany sighs, "Ah."

Fuad asks, "You were active politically, of
course?"

I laugh again. "I have no affiliation with any entity but life. You know what Karam Younis is like.
He and I are twins in spirit. People say in his case
that being brought up by a mother who was a prostitute has made him what he is. Well, I grew up in
a respectable family. So how do you explain our
similarity? Environment can't change natural gifts.
We despise respectability, both of us. The difference between us and other people, in fact, is that
we're honest and they're hypocritical."

"Are you going to write this drivel?" asks Umm
Hany, turning to Fuad.

"Fuad belongs to the same breed himself!"

"You're a real bastard," she bubbles gleefully.
"Don't you believe there are any decent people at
all?"

"Sure. Mr. Abbas Younis, for example, the au-

* A feddan is roughly equivalent to an acre.

thor of *Afrah al-Qubbah*. He's such an idealist, you know. That's why he throws his parents into jail and kills his wife and baby son!"

"What are you going to write?" Umm Hany asks Fuad.

"I'm not a lunatic like him," he says, guiding us to his Fiat.

We drive to the Citadel quarter. At the corner where our alley meets the main road, we get out of Fuad's car, unable to take it any further because of overflowing sewers. The stench accompanying us as we stumble over the crumbling pavement drives the drink from our heads.

Can the success I have now be sustained? Will I ever be able to escape from this slum, from this woman in her fifties who weighs a hundred kilos?

Tahiya and I had left the old house in the gravel market and were on our way to the theater, braving together the cold blast brought by the evening darkness, she with her black coat tightly wrapped around her voluptuous curves, I with the thought that her body was made for bed, not the theater, and that we were both in the wrong profession.

"I caught the boy during tea break sneaking hungry looks at you," I said.

"Abbas? He's only a kid."

"He's going to make an expert pimp someday."

"He has nice manners. And he's not to blame for what goes on in his house."

"He's Karam and Halima's son. And in these times what can you expect?"

I realize now that I hadn't understood at all what was going on in her mind.

"I never pictured you as the grieving lover," Sirhan al-Hilaly said with a chuckle.

"Did you ever imagine that one day we'd cross the Canal and win?"

"She's as poor as you are."

"Tell her—please . . ."

"You imbecile! She'd already decided to leave the stage. What's turned the trick is the fascination of marriage."

"Go to the devil! I'm almost out of my mind."

"You're angry, that's all."

"Believe me."

"The clever operator can't take a defeat!"

"It's not like that."

"That's all it is. Go back to Umm Hany right away, because you're not going to find anyone else to support you."

I hesitated before answering, "Sometimes I almost believe there is a God."

Sirhan guffawed. "Tariq son of Ramadan, even madness has its limits!"

Afrah al-Qubbah proves to be a real hit, with success confirmed night after night. Sirhan al-Hilaly has at last found the play that will enrich his theater, and the daily wage he agrees to pay me revives both body and soul.

Fuad Shalaby asks me, "Are you pleased with what I wrote about you?"

I press his hand gratefully. "After more than a quarter of a century I finally have my picture in your magazine."

"You'll never look back from now on. But did you know that Abbas has come out of hiding?"

"Really?"

"He paid a call on al-Hilaly yesterday at home. Do you know why?"

"Why?"

"He demanded a share of the profits."

I laugh so loudly that Amm Ahmad Burgal, behind the bar, almost jumps out of his skin. "Halima's son! What did al-Hilaly say to that?"

"He gave him a hundred pounds."

"Hell! He doesn't deserve it!"

"Abbas has no job and he's working on a new play."

"Bloodsucker! He'll never write anything new that's worthwhile."

"The future's in God's hands, not yours."

"Where was he hiding?"

"He didn't tell anyone."

"Fuad, my friend, aren't you convinced he's guilty?"

"Why would he kill Tahiya?"

"Because she confessed her infidelity."

He shrugs his shoulders and says nothing.

When I saw her coffin being hauled through the entrance of the apartment building, a terrifying sensation of emptiness slammed the pit of my stomach and spread until I felt my whole self turning to nothing. Then came an attack of weeping, catching me unawares. It was only my sobs that disturbed the other mourners. Even Abbas was dry-eyed.

I left in Sirhan al-Hilaly's car. "When I heard you crying," he said, "when I saw what you looked like, I almost burst out laughing, God help me."

"It surprised me, too."

I can't remember ever having seen you cry before."

I smiled. "Every racehorse has a tumble."

Death brings back memories of love and defeat.

The news arrives at the artists' coffeehouse where I always stop before leaving for the theater, and I rush to Sirhan al-Hilaly's room to ask if it's true.

"Yes," he says guardedly. "Abbas was staying in a pension in Helwan. He hadn't been seen for a long time. A suicide note was found in his room."

"Has his body been found?"

"No, they haven't found any trace of him."

"Did he give any reason for committing suicide?"

"No."

"Do you really believe he's killed himself?"

"Why should he have gone into hiding at exactly the time when success invites him to display himself along with his work?" There is a depressing silence. Then I hear him ask, "Why would he commit suicide?"

"For the same reason the hero of the play does."

"You're determined to accuse him."

"I challenge you to find any other reason."

Among artists and theater people the news spreads like wildfire. The usual measures, in such circumstances, are taken, but the search for Abbas uncovers nothing, at which I feel a deep sense of relief.

The success of this play, I say to myself, will be limitless.

KARAM YOUNIS

Autumn, "harbinger of winter cold." How will we be able to stand it? A lifetime peddling peanuts, melon seeds, and popcorn. And of this woman I've been sentenced to, like another imprisonment. In this country nearly everyone deserves to be locked up. Why single us out for jail? A law not founded on respect for its own workings is insane.

What are all these young boys going to do? What will happen to them? Wait till you see these old houses blown sky-high! A history reduced to rubble is pretty sad.

The woman never stops dreaming.

But what's this? Who is this? Some ghost from the past? "Bring me a poisoned dagger." What is it you want, you plague, you swamp of insects?

I turn to Halima and bark at her, "Look!" She jumps and we both speculate as to whether he's coming to congratulate us or to gloat, while he stands there grinning, with his little eyes, thick nose, and heavy jaws, like a pig. Be tough with him, the way you were the other times.

"Tariq Ramadan! What brings you here?"

"Our first visit from a loyal friend," Halima

47

sneers, "since we returned to the face of the earth!"
She's agitated, unnerved.

"I couldn't help it. I've been in a whirl, too."

"You're like a nightmare," I say, turning my
back on him to busy myself with a customer.

"I have bad news," he says.

"Bad news doesn't mean a thing to us," says
Halima.

"Even if it's about Mr. Abbas Younis?"

"He's a devoted son," I snap back. "When I refused to return to my old job at the theater, he set
us up in this little shop."

"And his play's been accepted," the woman adds.

But it's precisely about Abbas's play that Tariq's
come here. Has jealousy driven him crazy? He'd
rather die than see Abbas succeed. So let his jealousy kill him. He's the source of all our trouble.
No one can understand you better than I, Tariq: we
both crawled out of the same dung heap.

"The setting is this house," Tariq persists. "It's
about you, and it reveals other crimes no one ever
imagined."

Is that possible? Abbas never said a word about
the subject to anyone. But then he's such a perfect
little moralist. "What do you mean?" I ask.

"Everything. Everything! Don't you want to
know about it?"

What's he getting at? Why should Abbas com-
promise himself? "Even prison?" I ask.

48

"And that he's the one who denounced you to the police and that he killed Tahiya."

"That's nonsense!"

"What do you mean?" the woman shouts. "You hate Abbas!"

But he's said enough already to disturb me deeply. "Isn't it just a play?" I say feebly.

"Abbas can explain everything," Halima says.

"Go see the play for yourselves!"

"You've been blinded by hate!"

"Not by hate. By the crime!"

"You're the only criminal! You're crazy with spite!"

"My son may be stupid, but he is neither an informer nor a murderer," I retort, hiding my anxiety.

"Tahiya's murderer must be brought to justice!" he yells.

He and the woman begin a terrific row, but my own thoughts wander, until I finally get rid of him with a curse.

It is then that I find myself drowning in a sea of suspicion. Would Tariq have taken the trouble to come out this way to tell tales about Abbas that were groundless? The man is vicious, but he's not stupid. When my doubts finally get the better of me, I glance at the woman, only to find her staring back at me.

We live together in this old house like two strangers. If it weren't that Abbas would suffer, I'd divorce her. Abbas. The only thing that gives savor to this bitter life. He's the only hope I have left.

"He's lying," the woman mutters.

I feel much more concern than she does, almost to the point of being sympathetic with Tariq. "Why should he lie?"

"He still hates Abbas."

"But there's the play, too," I venture.

"We don't know anything about it. Go and see Abbas."

"Yes, I'll certainly go and have a talk with him."

"But you aren't making any move!" Stupidity and stubbornness can make Halima quite intimidating.

"There's no great rush."

"He has to know what's going on behind his back."

"And if he confesses?"

"What do you mean?"

"What if he admits that his play really does say what that swindler claims it does?"

"You'll get an explanation for everything."

"I wonder!"

"A real murderer doesn't expose himself."

"I don't know."

"Go see him, that's the main thing!"

"Of course I'll go."

"Do you want me to go?"

"You haven't got anything fit to wear," I point

out, reminding her how they'd seized all our money and how that son of a bitch of a detective beat me. "But that's all in the past. It's finished. We've got to concentrate on what happens to us now."

"That cheap swindler. He's lying."

"Abbas just couldn't accept our way of life, could he? So virtuous! You'd think he was a bastard, not my son! But he's always been loyal to us. And why would he kill Tahiya?"

"You're asking me?"

"I'm thinking aloud."

"You believe what the wretch said!"

"And you believe him, too."

"We've got to hear what Abbas has to say."

"As a matter of fact, I don't believe him."

"You're raving."

"Damn you!"

"I was damned the day I got tied to you."

"The same applies to me."

"I used to be pretty."

"Did anyone else want you but me?"

"Everyone always wanted me! Just my bad luck, that's all."

"Your father was a postman, but mine was employed on the Shamashirgi family estate."

"Which means that he was a servant."

"I come from a family."

"What about your mother?"

"Just like you."

"You're a windbag. You don't want to go, do you?"

"I'll go when it suits me."

Collecting my wits, I decide that, come what may, nothing worse can happen to us. To think that when this woman and I came together for the first time it was with feverish passion, beautiful dreams! What's happened to us? I'll have to make this trip. Some afternoon. That'll be the best time.

I don't know anything about the place where my son is supposed to be living. After his marriage we lost contact and we've had nothing to do with each other since. He despised us and rejected our way of life, and I despised and disowned him. When he moved to Tahiya's apartment I was glad not to see his scornful looks anymore. But now I'm running to him. It's the only hope left. When we came out of prison he treated us with understanding, as a dutiful son should. How can he be the one who threw us into it?

I go up to the porter at Tahiya's address a few days later to inquire about Abbas, only to be told that he left a couple of hours earlier, carrying a suitcase.

"Is he traveling somewhere?"

"He told me he'd be away for some time."

"Didn't he leave an address?"

"No."

This unexpected obstacle upsets me. Why didn't he tell us? Have Tariq's accusations reached him? I decide to look up Sirhan al-Hilaly at the theater in Sharia Imad al-Din. I ask to see him and he lets me in immediately, standing up to welcome me, full of sympathy over my safe homecoming: "If it weren't for my circumstances, I'd have come to see you and offer congratulations."

"Sirhan Bey," I say coolly, "that excuse is unacceptable."

He laughs. Nothing fazes him. "You're right."

"Our association has been a long one. A lifetime. My lifetime as prompter of your company. And you had the use of my house. Until I was arrested."

"I haven't treated you right," he mumbles. "How about a cup of coffee?"

"No coffee, no tea. I've come to see you about Abbas, my son."

"You mean the controversial playwright? His work is going to be an unprecedented success. And you, Karam, above all people, should understand how I feel."

"Good. But I didn't find him at home. The doorman told me he'd left carrying a suitcase."

"And why are you so upset about that? He's started on a new play. Who knows? Perhaps he's found a quiet place . . ."

"I've heard things about the plot of the play and I'm afraid it's got something to do with his leaving."

"Don't get the wrong idea, Karam."

"Tariq is malicious, and he . . ."

"Don't talk to me about Tariq," he interrupts. "I know him better than you. There's no need whatever to worry about your son."

"I'm afraid he may have . . ." I leave the sentence unfinished.

"The play is a fantasy. And even if it were true . . ."

"Tell me what you really think."

"I don't bother my head, not for one minute, about anything but the play itself. Any crime the hero commits onstage is good for the play. That's all that concerns me."

"But doesn't he betray his parents and kill his wife?"

"And a very good thing, too."

"What do you mean?"

"The elements of tragedy!"

"Don't you believe that's what actually happened?"

"It's got nothing to do with me." He shrugs.

"I want to know the truth."

"The truth is, we have a great play. And I am, as you know, the owner of a theater, not a public prosecutor."

"And I am in agony."

Al-Hilaly laughs. "What are you talking about? You never loved him!"

"The present isn't the past. You should understand that better than anyone else."

"A play is just a play. Nothing more. Otherwise the law would have the right to put ninety percent of our authors in the prisoner's dock."

"You don't want to offer me any comfort."

"I wish I could. Karam. Don't get worked up over absurd conjectures. No one could share them with you anyway except your most intimate friends. As for the public, they won't look beyond the play itself. By the way, why did you turn down your old job as prompter?"

"Thanks for asking. Abbas suggested that, and he told me you'd agreed. But I have no wish to go back to the past."

Al-Hilaly laughs again. "I can see that. You're your own boss now. And perhaps you make more money from the shop. That's all right, my friend. But don't get upset over Abbas. He's trying to establish himself. He'll surface at the proper time."

Our meeting is over and I take my leave, weighed down by contempt for all mankind and thinking: *No one cares about me, and I care for no one.* I don't even love Abbas, though my hopes are pinned on him. A treacherous murderer. Why should I blame him, though? I'm just like him. His outer paint has been peeled off, and he's shown the true colors he's inherited from his father—the naked self everyone pretends to honor these days, revealed without hypocrisy. What is goodness but mumbo jumbo, empty words said over and over in the theater and the mosque? There are pickup joints and rooms by the hour all along the Pyramids Road. How could he get me thrown into prison?

Who's this? At the door of the cafeteria I run into Tariq Ramadan, who holds out a slimy hand. I refuse it and tell him to get out of my sight.

I didn't do anything wrong. Drugs were chic, weren't they? And I was a man with no inhibitions. I followed my instincts, that's all. Other men were no different from me. What happened later was bad luck. Halima would say to me, "Do you expect my salary by itself to be enough to support your family?"

"You want a quarrel? I'm ready."

"Opium ruins everything."

"So what?"

"What about your son? Such a wonderful boy deserves to be looked after."

It wasn't my fault. My mother taught me what's right, instilled the fundamental principles. Halima wanted to play at being respectable, to forget the way she used to live. But I won't tolerate hypocrisy in my household.

"If you have trouble finding a suitable place sometimes," I said to al-Hilaly, "you can use my house." He gave me a searching look. "In the heart of Bab al-Shariya," I assured him, "even the jinn wouldn't suspect it!"

I was right. The old house took on new life: it was cleaned from top to bottom and the largest room was transformed into a salon for the hell-raisers. Those aristocrats. Those playboys—al-Agrudy, Shalaby, Ismail, Tariq—and Tahiya the playgirl. I respected them. They did as they liked without hypocrisy. There was a storeroom for snacks, drinks, and drugs, and Halima really took to the trade. A total hypocrite. I despise hypocrisy. Her true nature came right to the fore: the expert mistress of a new establishment, pretty, sharp-witted, as open-minded as I was and even more so, quite adept at running a brothel. The sky rained down gold.

What made the boy look at us in disgust? *Whose son are you anyway? Who's your father? Who's your mother? Who's your grandmother? You're a bastard, you are—offspring of a theatrical marriage!* An idiot, taken in by hypocrisy.

"The boy's sorrow is killing him," Halima sighed.

"Let him die of grief, the way every idiot should."

57

"He refuses to accept the situation."

"I don't like that word *accept*."

"He deserves some sympathy."

"He deserves to be throttled."

As he grew to hate me, my love for him was likewise uprooted. "Understand your life! Live in the real world! It's only the chosen few who have as good a life. Look at the neighbors! Don't you hear about what's going on around you? Don't you understand? Who are you anyway?" His eyes gave off a queer look, as if he lived outside the walls of time. What did he want?

Listen, I'll give you some advice: Your grandfather built this house. I don't know anything about him. Your grandmother—a young widow no different from your mother—made it a lovers' nest. Your father grew up in the bosom of reality. I'd really like to tell you everything. Should I be scared of you? If your grandmother hadn't died suddenly she would have married the master sergeant and lost the house. After she died he wanted to lord it over me. I beat him up and he tried to get me drafted into the old regular army, but the house stayed mine. It was Umm Hany—my mother's cousin and al-Hilaly's pimp—who got me the job as prompter. I'd like to lay these facts before you someday so you'll know what you came from, so you can trace your origins back to their roots without any sham reluctance. Be like your father, and love will unite us the way it used to when you were small. Don't be misled by your mother's hypocrisy. Someday you'll find out everything. Should I be afraid of you, son?

Back at the shop I have to face Halima's dreary questioning. What had Abbas told me? she wants to know.

"I didn't see him. He left the flat with a suitcase, and no one knows where he went."

She beats her thighs with her fists. "No one knows! Why didn't he let us know?"

"He doesn't think about us."

"He's the one who helped us start this shop."

"He wants to forget us now. As far as he's concerned, we belong to a past that's best forgotten."

"You don't understand my son. You should've gone to see al-Hilaly!" Exasperation makes me speechless, and she goes on: "You're not careful!"

"I'd like to bash your head in."

"Have you gone back on opium?"

"Only government ministers can afford it these days!" I retort. "Al-Hilaly doesn't know where he is either."

"You visited him?"

"He has no idea where he is," I repeated.

"My God! Did he move out of his flat?"

"No."

"He'll come back. Maybe there's a woman involved."

"That's what a woman like you would think."

"You don't care about him at all!" she screams. "You don't care about anyone but yourself!"

"I have been condemned to leave one prison for another."

"I'm the one who's living in a prison cell!"

The woman begins to sob, and that makes me even more exasperated. How could I ever have loved her? I wonder.

The red cafeteria. Walls and ceiling painted deep red, tablecloths and a thick carpet of the same color. I sat down at the barman's counter on a high leather stool, next to a young woman I hadn't noticed at first. Amm Ahmad Burgal, the barman, brought me the usual fava beans and a sandwich with a cup of tea and inevitably I glanced sideways, to be instantly dazzled by a young creature of extraordinary beauty. It struck me that she must be an employee of the theater, like myself, since the public wouldn't show up at the theater until well after eight o'clock. I heard Amm Ahmad ask her, "Any news about a flat, Miss Halima?"

"Searching for gold is easier," she replied, in a voice that oozed honey.

"Are you looking for a flat?" I butted in, bewitched.

She nodded, took a sip of tea, and Amm Ahmad

introduced us. "Mr. Karam Younis, the company's prompter. Miss Halima al-Kabsh, the new cashier."

"Getting married?" I said with my usual brashness.

Amm Ahmad answered for her. "She's living with an aunt in a cramped little apartment and dreams of having a small place of her own. But there are the problems of rent and key money."

"I have a house," I piped up at once.

She turned to me, interested for the first time. "Really?"

"A large house. It's old, but it has two floors."

"Is each floor an apartment?"

"No. It isn't divided into flats."

Amm Ahmad asked me if she could have a floor to herself.

"Of course she could." She asked if that wouldn't inconvenience the family. "I live there alone," I replied, at which she raised her eyebrows and turned away, prompting me to explain, in defense of my good intentions: "You and your family would find yourselves quite safe there."

She made no comment, but Amm Ahmad asked me, "What's the rent?"

"No one's ever taken it before. I'm not at all greedy."

"Shall I bring you a tenant?" he inquired solicitously.

"Oh no, I don't want that. It's the family house and it has its memories. I just wanted to help out the young lady, since we both work here in the theater."

Amm Ahmad laughed. "Give us a chance to think about it."

The young woman went out, leaving me charged with pangs of desire.

There she is now, sitting bent over in her chair with her arm folded, disgust and anger in her eyes, her forehead knitted in a scowl like a curse. Wouldn't it be better to live alone than share a life of wrangling? Where is the old enchantment—the sparkle, the foaming intoxication? Where in this world has its mummified corpse been interred?

Whenever I saw her in the red cafeteria I'd say to myself, "This girl grabs me like hunger." I'd imagine her and her high spirits in the old house, the way it would be rejuvenated, warmed. I fantasized about her curing me of deep-seated ills.

Amm Ahmad Burgal kept encouraging me in private. "Halima is a relative of mine," he said one day, "on my mother's side. She's educated and she's clever. I'm the one who got her her job here with al-Hilaly Bey."

"She's a wonderful girl," I responded, encouraging him to go on.

"Her aunt's a good woman. She herself is a very virtuous girl."

"There's no question about that."

His smile was so promising that it ignited my feelings, which were already pretty volatile; and I let myself surrender to the enticements of my own imagination, allowed myself to be lulled into daydreams, overpowering visions of sweet sensation, unbearably sustained. One day I finally said to him, "Amm Ahmad, I sincerely want . . ."

The rest of my unfinished sentence he understood. "Good for you!" he mumbled, full of glee.

"I have no income except my salary, but I own the house, and that's not something to be sneered at these days."

"Having a roof over your head is more important than keeping up appearances." And a little later that same week he was able to meet me with the words "Congratulations, Karam!"

During the days that followed, I floated on the tenderness of a tranquil engagement, wrapped in a veil whose silk translucence was woven from gossamer dreams and only the most dulcet of realities. The leather shaving kit she gave me made me so pleased that I felt like a child. Sirhan al-Hilaly raised my salary by two pounds and congratulated me on entering a new life. The theater people gave a party for us in the cafeteria and saw us off with flowers and sweets.

What's on the woman's mind? Her veined hand toys absentmindedly with a heap of popcorn. She

hasn't a cheerful thought in her head. We're condemned to venting our mutual irritation on each
other alone. We live in a prison cell. Only the light
streaming down on the rubbish strewn along this
ancient street makes it look a little different, as
gusts of wind pick up the lighter bits, blowing them
here and there to be kicked about by the feet of
countless boys. What's on the woman's mind?

On our wedding night, with a cock crowing on
a neighboring rooftop, she made the revelation that
dragged us both to the edge of a bottomless pit,
down which everything seemed to plunge but history itself. My first bewilderment turned to a numbness so deep that except for hearing the sound of
her choking sobs, I almost thought I'd died. The
sobs said everything. "I'll never forgive myself,"
she whimpered. *Really?* "I should have. . . ." *What
for? There's no need to say any more.* "But I loved
you," she murmured a second time.

I'd found out her secret. But she hadn't yet found
out mine. How could she know that her man had
likewise come to her with something of a past? Or
even understand how wild I'd been? I'd had a nasty
surprise, but her deception didn't bother me, and
even my surprise, once the numbness wore off,
seemed silly. "The past doesn't matter to me," I
declared heroically.

She bent her head, in what looked like grateful
humility.

"I hate the past," she said. "I'm becoming a new person."

"That's good," I said magisterially. Any desire to learn more I put aside. I was neither angry nor glad. I loved her. I entered into my new life with all my heart.

Hours go by, and we don't exchange a word. We're like two peanuts in a shell. Every customer complains about the rise in prices, the overflowing sewers, the exhausting queues at the government food stores, and we exchange condolences. Sometimes they look at the woman and ask, "What makes you so silent, Umm Abbas?"

What have I got left to look forward to? She, at least, expects Abbas to return.

I began my married life with genuine ardor. Halima announced the news of her approaching motherhood, and I was annoyed at first, but it was only a passing feeling. When Abbas was a child I loved him passionately.

Then things began to change. It was Tariq Ramadan who came up to me one day and said, "Hamlet's a tough role. Why don't you dissolve this in a cup of tea?" That was the beginning of a mad course. The man who cared about nothing was taken in. As time passed, the springs of life dried up and finally all joy was throttled in the grip of a crisis.

"Is this what you want? To blow your earnings

on poison and leave me to face life on my own?"
Halima's voice was now as disgusting to me as the
stench of backed-up sewers. We'd become like two
bare trees. Hunger was knocking at the old house's
door.

I was relieved to be able to say to her one day,
"The end is in sight."

"What are you talking about?"

"We'll fix up the east room upstairs as a place
for entertainment."

"What?"

"They'll come every night. We won't have to
worry about being poor anymore."

She gave me a look that boded ill, so I said, "Al-
Hilaly, al-Agrudy, Shalaby, Ismail. You know. But
we have to organize something that will keep them
coming."

"That's a dangerous game."

"But it's a very shrewd one. The profits will be
incredible."

"Isn't it enough for us that Tariq and Tahiya are
staying here? We're sinking to the lowest depths."

"We are rising to new heights. You and your
son can both shut up."

"My son's an angel. He's the one I'm worried
about."

"Just let him try defying his father, damn him.
You're ruining him with your silly ideas."

She gave in, but with resentment. She'd forgotten her wedding night. It's strange: people always yearn to be free of government regulations, but they're delighted to load shackles on themselves.

Here she is returning from her mission. Except for her services in the house, I'd have wished she'd never come back. There's disappointment in her face and I don't ask her any questions, ignoring her until finally she sighs, "His apartment is still locked up." I'm glad to have a customer. It's an excuse to avoid her. When he's gone, she hisses at me, "Do something."

My mind isn't with her: it's busy pondering how the government could throw us into prison for doing what it practices itself quite openly. Don't they operate gambling houses? Don't they promote brothels for their guests? I'm full of admiration for them. It isn't operations like that that drive me to rebel. It's the hypocritical injustice.

"Go and see al-Hilaly again," the woman says in a louder voice.

"Go yourself!" I say sarcastically. "You know him better than I do."

"God have mercy on your mother!" she says, stung to fury.

"At least she wasn't a hypocrite like you."

Then she sighs, "You don't love your son. You never loved him."

"I don't like hypocrites. But then, again, I don't deny he helped us."

She turns her back on me, muttering, "Where are you, Abbas?"

Where's Sirhan al-Hilaly? He'd gone out and hadn't come back. He was hardly likely to have gone to sleep in the bathroom. Meanwhile the gambling was still going on, and I was raking my percentage of the winnings after every round. Wasn't it time for Halima to serve drinks? Where was she? "Where's our producer?" I asked.

Everyone was busy with his cards and no one answered me. Was Tariq giving me a funny look? Halima should bring the drinks. "Halima!"

No answer. I couldn't leave my place or I'd be robbed. "Halima!" I shouted at the top of my voice. A little while later she appeared.

"Where were you?"

"I fell asleep."

"Make some drinks. And take my place until I come back."

I left the card room. Downstairs I found Abbas. "What woke you up at this hour?" I asked him.

"I couldn't sleep."

"Have you seen Sirhan al-Hilaly?"

"He left the house."

"When?"

"A while ago. I don't know exactly when."

"Did your mother see him?"

"I don't know?"

Why had he left? Why was the boy looking at me so quietly, with such despair in his eyes? I smelled something fishy. I may be many things, but I'm not a sucker. When there was nothing left in the house but cigarette butts and empty glasses, I gave the woman a long accusing look and then confronted her: "What went on behind my back?" Staring back disdainfully, she ignored my question altogether. "Did Abbas see?" She still didn't answer, and her silence irritated me all the more. "He's the one," I said, "who gave you the job. Everything has its price, that's what concerns me." She stamped her feet with fury. "As for you, though," I went on, "you aren't worth being jealous over."

"You're the lowest kind of vermin," she snarled, marching off to her room.

I guffawed. "Except for one little worm!"

She's returned from another outing. I hope you suffer more and go even crazier. Standing facing me in the shop, she says, "Fuad Shalaby is quite sure."

"Did you see him?"

"In the actors' coffeehouse."

"How does he know?"

"He said it's just an author's whim and that he'll show up at the right time with a new play in hand."

"A few words of comfort to a poor, infantile madwoman."

She dragged her chair into the farthest corner of the shop and sat there talking to herself "If God had only willed it! He could have given me better luck. But He threw me into the arms of a junkie."

"That's what happens to a man when he marries a whore."

"God have mercy on your mother! When Abbas comes back I'm going to live with him."

"I hope he returns, then, for my sake."

"Who'd ever imagine you're his father?"

"Any boy who's killed his wife and thrown his own parents in jail is my son and I'm proud of him!"

"He's an angel. And he's the product of my up-bringing."

I wish she'd talk herself into a straitjacket.

The karate chop that detective gave me on the neck. The punch that made my nose bleed. The raid was like an earthquake. It flattened everything, even Sirhan al-Hilaly: he was so frightened he just stood there blinking. And the savings we'd sold our souls for—confiscated. My God, it was awful!

What the devil was going on out in the hall?

I left my room to find Tariq and Abbas fighting, and Halima screaming.

"What's this nonsense?" I roared.

"It's ludicrous!" Tariq shouted. "Mama's boy is going to marry Tahiya!"

Everything seemed ludicrous, alien, incompatible with the euphoria beginning to rise from the drug I'd just taken.

"What kind of lunacy is this?" Halima shouted. "She's ten years older than you!"

Tariq spat out threats so vehemently that saliva was sprayed in every direction.

"Don't make matters worse," *Halima pleaded.*

"I'll bring destruction on this house," *Tariq shouted,* "and everyone in it!" *Whatever excitement I could have felt had receded. All I could muster was scorn and indifference, but before I could express anything, Halima told Tariq to take his clothes and get out.*

"Behind my back!" *he yelled.* "In this filthy house!"

"It's your presence that makes it filthy," *came my rejoinder, in so calm a tone that it sounded very strange in this stormy atmosphere. He didn't bother to look at me.*

Then Halima asked Abbas, "Is it true, what he says?"

"We've reached an understanding," *said Mama's boy.*

"Why weren't you considerate enough to consult us?" *I said with lofty indifference and, getting no response, went on:* "Will her salary be sufficient for running a home?"

"I'm going to take your place as the company's prompter."

"From author to prompter?"

"There's no inconsistency between the two."

"My son's gone mad!" *cried Halima convulsively. Then she told Tariq,* "Don't you act like a crazy fool, too."

He began making threats again, whereupon she yelled, "Get out of our house!"

"I'll stay here until Doomsday!" *came his parting shot. Exit Tariq, leaving the scene to the Noble Family. I looked maliciously from one to the other, enjoying myself.*

"I don't even know her except as this or that person's mistress," Halima said to Abbas, imploring him to reconsider.

I roared with laughter. "Your mother's an expert. Listen and take note!"

She went on pleading with him. *"Your father, as you well recognize, has become a good-for-nothing. You're our only hope."*

"We'll begin a new life," said Abbas.

I laughed. "Why have you deceived us all this time with your high-flown morality?"

Abbas strode out, and she broke into sobs. In the depths of my heart I would welcome his final departure, exulting over the collapse of the alliance between him and his mother against me. His had always been a dissenting voice, and I was fed up with him. Let him leave, and the house would become calm and harmonious. I'd even been afraid of him at times. He personified the meaning of words I hold in contempt, the nature of acts I abhor.

Halima was bewailing her fate. "Alone! Alone!"

"Alone! Don't pretend to be what you are not. In what way are we different? The same source, the same life, the same final goal!"

She stared at me with eyes that spoke loathing and contempt, then went to her room, with my loud, disdainful laugh following her all the way.

I look at her back over the mounds of peanuts, melon seeds, popcorn, and dried chickpeas heaped up in their bins along the counter. What kind of

existence is this, so totally joyless, in this atmosphere laden with smoke and aversion? The boy's
return and his success should have been enough to
give her new life.

*For once, I was really feeling quite cheerful, while Hal-
ima was hiding her gloom.*

*Sirhan al-Hilaly had been asking, "Where are Tariq
and Tahiya?"*

"A severe shortage of players," said Salim al-Agrudy.

*I laughed. "Exciting news, Sirhan Bey: my crackpot
son has married Tahiya."*

*The whole table burst out laughing. "It appears," said
Ismail, "that your son is a real artist."*

"The kid," exclaimed al-Hilaly.

"The marriage of the season!" added Shalaby.

*"You'll now find Tariq," said Ismail, "wandering in
the desert, like Magnun Layla."**

The table burst out laughing again.

*"But Halima isn't joining in our happiness," observed
Sirhan.*

*"Halima is at a funeral," she said, and went on mix-
ing drinks.*

*"Who knows? Perhaps he's found the happiness that
evades the rest of us."*

"In spite of everything!" I laughed out loud.

---

* Refers to the theme of a love lyric by Gameel (d. 701), a poet from Medina.
Magnun was the self-immolating lover and Layla his ever-inaccessible ina-
morata.

"These days only mules are lucky enough to be happy," Halima said bitterly.

"Will he go on trying to write plays?" said Sirhan.

"Of course," Halima replied.

"Great. Tahiya will be able to supply him with lots of useful experience."

After that I became absorbed in collecting the money. It was the first night I'd done business with no one to spy on me and I thoroughly enjoyed it.

The woman is out searching for her son. Alone in the shop, I wonder what kind of end he's assigned her in the play. I forgot to ask about that. Has he lowered the curtain over the time we spent in prison? Over this shop? Customers come one after another. These people don't realize how much I despise and detest them. Hypocrites! They carry on exactly the same way we did, then offer up prayers at the proper times. I'm better than they are. I'm liberated. I belong to the good old days, before religion and moral behavior became all the rage. I'm beseiged in this shop, though by an army of hypocrites, every man and woman. The state, too. That's why it neglects the sewers, leaves us to line up in queues, and deluges us with bombast. And my son gives me a splitting headache with his silent reprimands, then commits betrayal and murder. If only I could get hold of a little opium. It would make everything bearable. Why were we so beguiled at the time of our engagement? Why did it whisper to us so insinuatingly of a sweetness that didn't exist?

"I am indebted to Amm Ahmad Burgal for a joy that is almost more than a man can bear."

"Don't exaggerate."

"Halima, who can be happier than a man whose heart has not beaten in vain?" Her radiant smile was like a flower in full bloom.

Where does she hide this sweetness now?

Ah, if only it were possible to go back in time as it is to go back in space. Somewhere in my primeval being is a soft spot that makes me want to cry over these ruins. Somewhere a Karam who no longer exists is weeping over the Halima of the past.

The woman has returned. She comes in and sits down without even a nod at me. I ignore her completely, and she doesn't speak, but her eyes look serene. What has she found out? She's no doubt withholding good news from me, the sow: if it were bad news she'd have poured it over my head the minute she came in. Has Abbas returned? I refuse to ask. Several minutes pass before she says, "We're invited to see the play!" She hands me a printed notice.

My eyes come to rest on the name of the author: Abbas Younis. I'm carried away with pride. "Shall we go?"

"What a question!"

"We may get a shock when we see ourselves."

"What matters is that we see Abbas's play," she says. "My heart tells me that the playwright is bound to appear."

"Who knows?"

"My heart knows."

We do our best to look presentable: I wear a suit that isn't too bad, and Halima has rented a *tailleur* from Umm Hany. At the theater they receive us graciously.

"But I don't see the playwright," Halima says.

"He didn't come," says Sirhan al-Hilaly, "but I've told you enough." So she's met him and managed to get considerable news from him.

Since we're early, we go to see Amm Ahmad Burgal, who gives us each—on the house—a sandwich and a cup of tea. "It's like old times," he remarks, but we neither smile nor comment. At curtain time we take our seats in the front row. The theater is packed.

"It's a success," observes Halima.

"You can't judge until a week's gone by." Despite the ironic detachment I feel—how can I take a play seriously when life itself does not mean anything to me?—my nerves are on edge.

Ah, the curtain is rising—to reveal our house. Our house, no other. Was it al-Agrudy or Abbas who wanted it this way? The father, the mother, and the son. A brothel and a gambling den, that's what it is. There's more than crime and betrayal there. The stage mother is an uncontrollable whore, her relations with the director, the producer, the critic, and Tariq Ramadan follow one after another: and I look swiftly at Halima, whose breath is coming in rough gasps. It's sheer hell. Now you can wallow in your son's opinion of you. What he thinks of his father and mother is painfully clear. Who would have imagined that his serene head could hold all this devastation? I'm glad he sees his mother this way, glad he's come out with what he really thinks of her. This piece of drama is his way of wreaking vengeance on me, punishing me for what I am.

But in this moment of scandal I experience a sense of triumph over both the mother and the son, over my two mortal enemies. He doesn't understand me. He presents me as someone fallen, a man who has resorted to corruption in reaction to the challenge of reality. I'm not like that, you fool. I never had any stature to lose. I grew up untamed and free, watching the hypocrites, learning from them. That's what you cannot understand. What's the secret of your success? You flatter them, you pander to their sense of superiority. I spit on you and your evasions!

Thunder of wild applause.

We're invited—as is customary—to the party in

the cafeteria, in celebration of a successful play. "Shall we join them or leave?" I whisper.

"Why shouldn't we join the party?" *It's no use pretending to be above it all, Halima. You don't have the same wings I have.* "He didn't need to commit suicide," she murmurs.

"What kind of an end did you expect for a murderer?" I ask, hoping to nettle her.

"He got a lot of sympathy."

Sirhan al-Hilaly declares loudly, "My intuition says that it won't be a flop," and they begin drinking toasts.

"It's brutal, of course," says Salim al-Agrudy, "but it's impressive."

"It reminds the audience of their everyday hardships," says Fuad Shalaby. "But it's terribly pessimistic."

"Pessimistic?" scoffs al-Hilaly.

"He needn't have committed suicide. The audience's hopes and aspirations were all pinned on him."

"Don't look at it as a suicide," answers al-Hilaly. "It's just a way out for the new generation."

"God protect all bastards!" roars al-Hilaly. And turning to Tariq Ramadan, he raises his glass and says, "To the revelation of a great actor, discovered in his fifties!"

"A discovery more significant," Fuad Shalaby exclaims, "than finding an oil well!"

Al-Hilaly turns to us for a response, but I antic-ipate him and raise my glass. "A toast to the absent playwright."

A surge of acclaim turns into a riot of drinking at the theater's expense. I revel in scandals recalled about every man and woman present. Why were we the only ones imprisoned? Friends, libertines— drink a toast to me! I am your true symbol!

When we return to the old house, it is dawn and we have no wish to sleep. I light the charcoal in the heater in the hall, where the tiles are covered by an old Assiut rug, and Halima and I sit down, as if, in spite of our mutual aversion, we want to be together for a while. Which of us will start the conversation? How very difficult it is for us to talk to each other. We are always on guard.

"Did you like the play?" I ask.

"Very much. Very much."

"And the subject?"

"What a silly question from someone who's spent a lifetime in the theater!"

"Why do we always deceive ourselves? There's no doubt about what he intended."

"I won't accept this silly way of thinking!"

"It was even more true than the real facts."

"There's no connection between the way I ap-pear in that play and the real facts." I can't help chuckling at that, which annoys her. "It's just a fantasy."

"All of them just as we know them in real life?"

"An author is free to do as he likes, to keep some characters as they are in real life and change others, as he wishes. There were completely new elements in the plot."

"Why did he portray you as he did?"

"That's his business."

"I thought he loved and respected you!"

"There's no doubt about that."

"You give yourself away with that bitchy look of yours!"

"I know I'm right."

"Even Tariq!" I say with contempt. "I never imagined you'd sink to such depths."

"Spare me your filthy thoughts."

"If it hadn't been for your fun and games on the side we'd have made a lot more money."

"What about you? The fact is that he shows you much better than you really are, which proves that he really was using his imagination." I laugh so loudly that she says, "Quiet! People returning from dawn prayer will hear you."

"So what? That strange boy of yours. He threw us into prison."

"How can you expect anyone to lead a decent life? You don't follow any rules but your own."

"But he claimed to be so perfect. That's what gave me a pain in the neck!"

"He's a wonderful boy. A well-known playwright. My son." Outwardly, at least, she's pleased with things.

"What I admire is his brutality!"

"When he comes back I'm going to leave this damn house and live with him."

"This house? Where every room bears witness to our past glory?"

She leaves me, and I sit there alone holding my hands over the heater. I'd like to know more about my father. Was he one of these hypocrites? He died young, my mother sank very low, and I grew up her way, under the devil's horns. But you, Abbas, are a dark horse.

How bored I am! I'm like a jinni shut up in a long-necked bottle. No room to maneuver.

I follow the play's success with fascination, expecting the playwright to surface, even to come up with a new play, hoping that his success will change the course of my tedious life.

I make frequent visits to the theater to nose around for news; and one morning as I enter Amm Ahmad Burgal rushes up to me and takes me into the empty cafeteria. His downcast face alarms me. I sense that behind it lies bad news.

"Karam! I was just about to come see you."

"Why! What's wrong?"

"Abbas."

"What about him? Say it, Amm Ahmad."

"He disappeared from the pension in Helwan,

the place where he was staying, and he's left a strange message behind."

"What message? Don't you want to tell me?"

"A note, saying he was going to commit suicide."

My heart sinks, pounding, like anyone else's. We look at each other silently. "Have they found . . . ?"

"No," he says. "A search is being made, though."

"Ah. Probably . . . who knows? But he wouldn't have written the note, would he, if he hadn't . . . ?" My mouth says the words, my thoughts are astray.

"May the Lord help you." He sounds like someone who believes the matter is ended.

"I must go to Helwan!"

"Sirhan Bey al-Hilaly has already gone."

A futile, painful trip. There is nothing but the suicide note. Abbas has vanished, disappeared once and disappeared again. Finding his body will be the only proof of his suicide. Would he have written the note if he hadn't really made up his mind to commit suicide?

"If he really wanted to commit suicide," al-Hilaly muses, "why didn't he do it in his room?"

"So you doubt the seriousness of his intentions?"

"Yes, I do."

I do not return to the old house until evening. Halima isn't there and I realize that she's gone to the theater to find out why I'm so late. I close up the empty shop and sit in the hall waiting for her. An oppressive hour goes by before she comes in, her eyes ablaze with madness. We gazed at each other for a second, then she cries, "No! Even if he wanted to kill himself he wouldn't do it! He couldn't! He couldn't kill himself! It's not possible!"

Sinking into a sofa, she bursts into wild tears, slapping her cheeks with both hands.

From the bowels of prison, born again to the face of the earth! Abbas's face appears before me, and I take him in my arms. Weighed down by shame and humiliation, I bury my face in his chest. "How badly we've treated you," I whisper. "I wish we'd died. Then you'd be rid of us."

"It's only your words that hurt me," he answers gently. I can't help weeping. "We should be thankful now," he says. "Let's think about the future."

"You're all alone, son. God has seen fit to take away your wife and child," I say, shaking with sobs, "and we weren't there to comfort you."

"What's past is past."

With his father he scarcely exchanges a word. We are all together in the hall of the old house the way we used to be, sometimes, in the old days.

"I beg you not to bring up the past," he says. Then, pausing for a moment, he goes on: "I've been thinking things over. Does Father want to go back to his old job in the theater?"

"No. Never, damn them!"

"I can turn the reception room into a shop. We'll sell some of the furniture and set up a snack shop.

It's an easy business and fairly profitable. What do you two think of that?"

"Just as you see it, son," I say with gratitude. "And I pray God that I may hear good news about you soon."

"I hope so. I think I'm about to come up with a winner."

I invoke God's blessing on him over and over, until he says, looking at us from one to the other, "What matters most is that you cooperate with each other and that I don't hear things that hurt me."

"I have often dreamed of living with you," I say with a sigh.

"If God means me to be successful, everything will change."

"Why don't you go ahead and take her with you!" Karam says, growling.

"You must cooperate with each other. I'll do all I can to give you a decent life, but you must learn to get along together."

What cooperation? The poor boy doesn't understand anything; he's too naive to comprehend the secrets of the heart even when they're displayed right under his nose. How can he understand what his father did when he's never seen anything but the man's melancholy exterior? My son can make sacrifices and be as generous as his devoted heart wants to, but doesn't he realize that he's shutting up two adversaries together in a single prison cell? From one prison to another, from loathing to sheer hatred. There's no hope for me, son, unless you can succeed, unless you can rescue me.

I glance at him as he works, selling peanuts, melon seeds, popcorn, and chickpeas, throwing the piasters into a half-open drawer. He wallowed so long in a life of sin that he's probably dreaming now about going back to the habit that prison cured him of. If it weren't for Abbas, his stipulation that we divide the earnings between us, we'd have been ruined again by now. That permanent look of melancholy he has! Except when customers come in, the gloomy mask never falls from his face. He's aged so much he looks older than he really is, and that means I've aged too. *The years in prison. The night of the raid when detectives kept slapping my face . . . Ah, the bastards, not one of them came to see us! Al-Hilaly is as big a bastard as Tariq Ramadan. Detained at the police station just one night and then released. We bore the punishment alone. Our neighbors say the law is only hard on the poor, and they accuse us and gloat over our misfortune. They do business with us, though. My only hope is that you succeed, son.*

Time passes. We have nothing to say to each other. The fire of hatred is stronger than the heat of an oven. *When I clean this hateful old house, or when I cook, I feel so miserable. Why am I condemned to this wretched life? I used to be pretty, all piety and decorum.*

Fate. Fate. Who will explain the meaning of fate to me? But God is on the side of the patient, the long-suffering. My destiny is in your hands, Abbas. I'll never forget your visit that night, on the feast of the birthday of Sidi al-Sharany,* and your words, which relieved my torment and opened up the gates of heaven: "My play has been accepted at last!"

I hadn't been so happy since he was a young boy. Even his father's face shone with joy. *What have you got to do with it? I don't understand. You hate him just as you hate me. All right, he has grown up to be a dramatist, contrary to what you predicted. To you his idealism was stupidity, but good will always out. His strength and energy will sweep away the dross of riffraff like you.*

I don't like autumn, except that it brings us closer to opening nights. *Where do they come from, these clouds that blot out the light? Isn't it enough that the clouds cover my heart?* I hear the man speaking to me:

"Look."

I see Tariq Ramadan coming toward the shop, looking as if he were someone bringing news of an accident in the street. *Has he come to congratulate us or to gloat over us?*

He stands there in front of us, his greeting lost in the empty air.

"Our loyal friend, paying us a visit for the very first time," I say.

* A holy man to whom a small local mosque was dedicated.

I pay no attention to his excuses until I hear him intone, "I have bad news."

"Bad news doesn't mean a thing to us."

"Even if it's about Mr. Abbas Younis?"

My blood turns cold, but I remain as calm as I can. "His play's been accepted," I say proudly.

"It's nothing but a deplorable joke. What do you know about the play!" He goes on to summarize it, citing the most important episodes, and ends by saying, "That's it—everything!"

Hiding my anxiety and with my head spinning, I reply, "What do you mean? You hate Abbas!"

"Go see the play for yourselves!"

"You've been blinded by hate."

"By the crime, you mean."

"The only criminal is you."

"Tahiya's murderer must be brought to justice!"

"You're a low-down crook yourself. Why don't you just get lost!"

"How can they say that prison teaches people manners?" he says, laughing sarcastically.

I grab a handful of chickpeas and throw them at him. He draws back jeering, then leaves.

What has Abbas written? What has he done? My son would never kill anyone or be disloyal; at least he wouldn't betray his mother. He's an angel.

The man and I look at each other. I must haul myself out of this unending loneliness. "Tariq is lying," I say.

"Why should he lie?"

"He still hates my son."

"But there's the play, too."

"Go and see Abbas!"

"I'll see him, sooner or later."

"But you aren't making any move."

"There's no great rush."

He exasperates me; like Tariq, he has no love for Abbas.

"He has to know what's going on behind his back!" I yell.

"And if he confesses?"

"You'll get an explanation for everything."

"I wonder!"

"A real murderer doesn't expose himself."

"I don't know."

"Go see him, that's the main thing!"

"Of course I'll go."

"Do you want me to go?"

"You haven't got anything fit to wear."

"Then it's up to you to go."

"That crook is lying."

"He detested the way we lived. He was so idealistic you'd think he wasn't my son at all, but someone else's bastard," the man says. Then he seems to change his mind. "But he didn't double-cross us. And why would he kill Tahiya?"

"You're asking me?"

"I'm thinking aloud."

"You believe what the wretch said!" I shout.

"You believe him, too."

I press my lips together to hold back the tears.

"We've got to hear what Abbas has to say."

"As a matter of fact, I don't believe him."

"You're raving!"

"Damn you!"

"I was damned the day I got tied to you!"

"The same applies to me."

"I used to be pretty."

"Your father was a postman, but mine was employed on the Shamashirgi family estate."

"Which means that he was only a servant."

"I come from a family."

"What about your mother?"

"Just like you."

"You're a windbag. You don't want to go, do you?"

"I'll go when it suits me." Then, changing his tone, he says, "He's most likely to be at home in the afternoon."

Praying for patience, I surrender to his indolence, though doubt is killing me from my feet upward. *What is it they say about the best people? A rose among the ruins—in a community of thieves and their victims. The man has bought me material to make a dress so I could go out, but I've put off making it. I'll start cutting it out right away and then see about getting it made. The son of a whore insults me about my origins.*

But Abbas could never betray his mother. He may have scorned everything else, but not my love. Love is stronger than evil itself.

My happy childhood home in al-Tambakshiyya, where the sun always shone, even in the winter, even at night, the home of Halima, beautiful daughter of a beautiful mother and a father who always brought home nice things, things we liked. "Let her go on," my mother used to say to him. "Education will give her the opportunity of a lifetime. I wish I'd had the chance." That was before he died.

Our good cousin, Amm Ahmad Burgal, came visiting one day, "The girl's father is dead, and keeping her on at school has become a hardship."

Mother asked, "So what should we do, Amm Ahmad?"

"She has a certificate, and she's clever. She must find work. They'll be looking for a cashier at the theater."

"Would that kind of work suit you?" asked Mother.

I answered with apprehension, "I suppose practice will make up for what I lack in experience."

"El Shamashirgi is a friend of al-Hilaly Bey. Your father never worked for him, but he's the biggest man in the district and he's been our benefactor. If you mention his name when you have your interview, I'll take care of the rest."

And thus I was poised, the first time I set foot in

the theater, to enter a different world. It was a marvelous place. It even had a special smell. Amm Ahmad shrank in stature: his work there was not very important. Summoned to meet the producer, I entered his magnificent inner sanctum in my old shoes and my simple white dress, and walked timidly, step by step, toward him. His tall frame, piercing eyes, and masterful expression made him almost awe-inspiring; and he scrutinized me at such length that I thought I'd nearly die. Finally, he gave me a sheet of paper to see how fast I could write the numbers.

"You'll need some practice before you can take over the job," he said in his domineering voice. "What's your name?"

"Halima al-Kabsh,"* I said shyly.

"Al-Kabsh!" The name made him smile. "What of it? You're a good deal more attractive than the actresses in our company. I'll want to examine you after you finish your training."

So I set to work in a burst of enthusiasm, inspired not by concern for my future, but by the wish to please that wonderful enchanter. I described him to my mother, and she said that was what the upper classes were like. If I could only win his approval, I thought, what a lucky break it would be for me.

* Al-Kabsh—the ram.

When I stood before him, I was panting. "You're the jewel of the company, Halima. God is beautiful and He loves beauty." At what point did he begin to fondle me? Sunlight piercing the window shone full in my face; out in the street someone was playing a dance on a rustic flute. Gasping, I shoved his huge hand away, and said, "No, sir. I'm a respectable girl." His laugh made my ears ring.

In the silence that ensued in that vast locked room, my protests expired. A rush of hot breath, a cunning approach, and all my determined resolutions were confounded. It was a nightmare of the kind that draws tears but wins no sympathy. In the world outside that room other people came and went. My mother died before she found out.

In the afternoon he gets a move on at last. My taut nerves relax a little. I'm clutching at a straw, but what can I expect? I've got to get the dress ready, just so I can do something. My son will tell his secrets to me, but not to that despicable man. What have I got left now except Abbas?

The disappointments came with—no, even before—the opium. My expectations—all dead and buried now—had been so sweet. I remember one night when he drained the dregs from his glass, leered drunkenly, pointed to the room next to the reception room, and said, "My mother used to go into that room alone with the master sergeant."

The disclosure was so brutal it shocked me. Abbas was tucked up in his cradle, asleep. I couldn't believe my ears. "You're drunk, Karam."

He shook his head. "She used to warn me to stay in my own room."

"That wasn't right."

He interrupted me. "I don't like hypocrisy. You're a hypocrite, Halima."

"God forgive her. Do you still feel resentful toward her?"

"Why should I hold it against her?"

"I don't understand you."

"Your husband is unrivaled among men. He doesn't believe in any man-made lies." *What does he mean? He's not a bad husband, but he makes fun of everything. He ridicules my faith, the things I hold sacred, my principles. Doesn't that man respect anything at all? He's just exposed his mother shamelessly.* "And that's lucky for both of us," he went on, "because if it weren't so, I'd have divorced you on our wedding night."

I was pierced to the heart and tears welled up in my eyes. I'd just received the second cruel blow of my life.

"You can't help it, Halima. When are you going to become liberated?"

"You're wicked and cruel."

"Don't bother using words like that. They don't mean anything."

He told me how his mother had been madly in love with the policeman, how she'd neglected him, and how he'd grown up "liberated," thanks to her dissipations. "I owe everything to her," he said finally, with a drunken leer.

He was like some frightful object hung around my neck. I was living with a force that had no principles. On what basis, then, was I to deal with him? The letdown came before the opium. The opium found no spirit left to crush.

When I catch sight of him coming back, my heart leaps in spite of its aversion. He looks even older in the street than he does in the shop. He sits down without looking at me and I can't help asking, "What did he say to you?"

"He left the flat with a suitcase, and no one knows where he went," he says without emotion.

Ah! What instant trepidation, instant torment! Is there no end to calamity?

"Why didn't he let us know?"

"He doesn't think about us."

Pointing to the four corners of the shop, I say, "He treated us better than we deserve."

"He wants to forget us now."

"You should have gone to see al-Hilaly."

He answers me with a look full of scorn and disgust, and I, to provoke him, tell him he doesn't know how to act.

"I'd like to bash your head in!"

"Have you gone back on opium?"

"Only government ministers can afford it these days." He lowers his voice. "Al-Hilaly doesn't know where he is either."

"You visited him?" I ask anxiously.

"He has no idea where he is."

"My God! Did he move out of his flat?"

"No."

"Maybe there's a woman involved."

"That's what a woman like you would think."

"What can I say to someone like you? You don't care about him at all."

My misery is too much for me. I weep bitter tears.

Wearing my new dress, an old shawl around my shoulders, and without any hope, I go to Abbas's building, where my despair is confirmed when I question the doorman.

"You must know something about what happened?"

"Nothing at all."

I don't have the courage to go to the theater. My reluctant footsteps direct me homeward. I stop on the way and visit Sidi al-Sharany to seek his miraculous help, then come back to my prison cell to find the man joking and laughing with a customer, quite unconcerned. I sit down defeated, my spirits at lowest ebb, my endurance gone. "Do something," I manage to say to him. "Don't you have any plan in mind?"

"I'd like to kill you; someday I will kill you!"

"Go and see al-Hilaly again."

"Go yourself," he interrupts. "He gives special attention to his slave girls."

"The truth is, I'm your mother's victim! My torture comes from her grave. She's the one who made you such a brute!"

"Compared with you, she was a decent woman."

This theater—where I'd been raped and no one held out a helping hand—was the backdrop of my torment and my love. While its lofty dome echoed with admirable sentiments, phrased in the sweetest way, my blood spilled on its comfortable seats, the blood of my secret, strangling me. I was lost, lost. He wasn't even aware of my adoration. Nothing mattered to him. He probably even forgot my name.

"You're avoiding me! I can't take any more. I have to see you."

"Is there anything you need?"

"What? Have you forgotten? I've lost everything!"

"Don't exaggerate. I don't like it. What happened isn't worth troubling your head over." Tears welled up in my eyes. "No," he said, "no. Nothing that goes on in this theater should ever be taken to heart."

"But what about me? Don't you see what it means to me? Don't leave me!"

"The whole thing is much simpler than you imagine. No harm done. Cheer up—for the sake of your work and your future. Forget what happened. It's no use asking me to keep remembering it."

He was as hard as granite. My aversion for him was as strong as my love had been. *Abandoned, alone, in torment. Someday my aunt would guess the secret of my suffering. What could I expect from a world that knows no God?*

Late in the afternoon I go to the actors' coffee-house, where I catch sight of Fuad Shalaby smoking a narghile and make a beeline for him. I may be the last person he's expecting to see, but he stands to welcome me and pulls up a seat for me.

"I should have come to visit you. Damn all the work!"

I ignore his words. "Nobody's visited us. Not that it makes any difference. I'm so upset over Abbas's disappearance that I had to come."

"There's no need to get upset." He smiles. "It's quite obvious he left to get away from spongers. It's a good thing he did. He's probably working on his next play."

"But he should have told me."

"Try to overlook his negligence. Don't worry. You're still as pretty as ever, Halima. How is Karam?"

"He's alive and active, pursuing his hobby of making mankind miserable."

He laughs, in a way that gets on my nerves, so much so that I get up and leave the coffeehouse.

This time I have the courage and the determination to go to the theater. I ask to see the producer and enter the room, the selfsame room—same leather couch, same man.

No, he's different: there's nothing left of the old self but the depravity, which seems to have aged him more than prison has us. *Which of us two is more to blame for my unhappiness?* He rises to greet me. "Welcome, welcome! I'm delighted to see you looking so well," he exclaims.

"Well?" I retort as I take a seat.

"As befits the mother of a successful playwright."

"At the moment, he's the cause of my suffering."

"That's suffering for no reason whatsoever. I have good news: He's contacted me by phone."

I interrupt, aflame with joy, "Where is he?"

"I don't know. That's his secret; let him keep it if he wants to. The important thing is that he's busy on a new play."

"Has he left his job?"

"Yes. It's a risk—but he's sure of himself, and I'm confident, too."

"He didn't bother to get in touch with me?"

"Well, he wants to avoid being interrogated about his play; that's what I think."

"Certain suspicions are being voiced, over and over. What do you think about it all?"

"A play is a work of art, and art is a fantasy, no matter how much it borrows from the truth."

"But what about people's assumptions?"

"The audience doesn't see anything in it. To think otherwise is idiocy, and if it weren't for Tariq's stupidity . . ."

"He's his enemy, damn him!" I interject.

"Now, I want you to cheer up!"

"I heard that Karam Younis is asking for your hand?"

"Yes, he is."

"The damage can be repaired."

"No, I refuse to go along with that kind of deception."

"You mean you're going to let him know the truth?"

"I think that's the best way."

"You're a remarkable girl! So many people are without principles these days. Are you going to tell him who it was?"

"That's not important."

"It would be better not to."

As I enter the cafeteria, Ahmad Burgal sees me and shouts, "Welcome!"

I sit in front of him, silent, while he begins to make a sandwich and tea for me. Just two people on this earth have brought about whatever happiness we have known: Ahmad Burgal and Umm Hany. Recollections come flooding in upon me: a cup of tea, a sandwich, a little flirtation, and the music of a flute heard in hell, like clear drops of rain falling on a pile of garbage.

Amm Ahmad says, "Abbas's success is a good omen. It'll make up for the past."

"But he's left without a word."

"Don't be upset. No one here is worried about it."

"And Tariq Ramadan?"

"He's half crazy."

I went through a terrible new ordeal. I'd been determined to confess—I was respectable and modest and I hated deception—but at the last moment I'd been silenced by fear. Karam seemed such a commendable young man, serious and loving. Would I lose him? Fear kept me silent until the door had closed on us. My weakness appalled me, I wept. The truth now stood between us, naked, taut, ready to serve any purpose. "I am a criminal," I whispered. "I just couldn't bring myself to tell you beforehand."

The grave look in his eyes baffled me. What I'd dreaded was taking place. "I was so afraid of losing you. You must believe me: I was raped."

I lowered my eyes, frightened by his agitation. I said things and he said things, but our words were lost in the intense heat of our agony. His voice was engraved on my consciousness: "The past doesn't matter to me." I cried all the more, but some unexpected ray of hope had appeared to me. I told him that he was gallant, that I would dedicate my life to making him happy. I dried my eyes. "How easy it is for the innocent to be lost," I whispered.

With a heavy heart, I return to the prison cell and sit down. I'll tell him about meeting Fuad Shalaby and nothing more. I won't offer him any relief. He doesn't love Abbas. He pretends to be quite disinterested in what I found out. If he only suffered as I do. The snacks we sell help other people while away the time, but our only distraction is exchanging abuses.

My letdown had continued step by step. A new vice was threatening the foundations of our home. "Opium is a terrible thing. It will destroy you." "I'm grateful for it, at any rate."

"You're running away from reality. And you're doing it faster and faster."

"Again, I say thanks to it."

"I'm doing my utmost. And there's Abbas to think about, your beloved son." He takes another sip of black tea. "My salary by itself isn't enough to keep the house going."

"You have the rent from Ramadan's room."

"And even that's not enough. Life is so expensive."

I understand you now. And I'm afraid of you. You aren't what I thought you were at the outset of our life together. You've lost everything, even the potency you used to boast about. We've moved into separate rooms. Between us there's neither love nor desire! You're the only thing left, Abbas. Pay no heed to what your father says. Don't believe him. He's sick. It's a good thing you're alone most of the time. God be with you—He is our sufficiency. Be an angel. Let your friends, your books, and the theater be your teachers. Be my son and the son of other good people. You're the only light in this old house steeped in darkness. Be unique in every way.

He steals a furtive glance at me now and again, hoping I might divulge what I know. Never. I'll challenge him to hate me more.

"Winter's coming. How can we stay in this open shop?" he says.

"When Abbas succeeds, our luck will change," I answer confidently.

"When Abbas succeeds!" he retorts, bitterness in every syllable.

"I'll go live with him," I say defiantly, "and he won't begrudge you an overcoat or a woolen cloak!"

The red cafeteria was always the same; it laughed at the shifts and changes in its patronage, hearing most of what was said, but believing no one. "Here's your sandwich. I'll get your tea ready," Amm Ahmad Burgal said.

A young man came and sat on the stool next to me. He ordered beans and a sandwich. He was one of the theater people, it appeared, but he wasn't one of the actors. A young man, attractive except for his large head and nose. Amm Ahmad asked me, "Any news about a flat, Miss Halima?"

In front of the stranger, I answered somewhat diffidently, "Searching for gold is easier."

"Are you looking for a flat?" the young man said abruptly.

I replied that I was, and Amm Ahmad introduced us.

"Getting married?" the young man went on to ask boldly.

Ah, the seduction's begun: Here in this theater it gets off the ground quickly and does not stop short of violence.

*The quarry is brought down to the accompaniment of a
native flute.*

"I own an old house that has two floors."

"Is each floor an apartment?"

"No. It isn't divided into flats."

Amm Ahmad asked him if I could have one floor
to myself, and he said I could.

"Won't that inconvenience the family?" I asked.

"I live there alone," he declared.

When I turned away from him, indignant at his
boldness, he went on cunningly: "You and your
family would find yourselves quite safe there."

I thanked him and said no more. *He hadn't made
a bad impression on me. What did he want? He knew
nothing about my tragedy, my love, or my distrust of
mankind.*

I say that I'm going to Umm Hany's small flat in
al-Imam, where Tariq Ramadan is staying. She re-
ceives me warmly, but I have to wait until Tariq
gets up. He comes out of his room with his hair
standing on end, looking like the devil.

"Welcome," he remarks, with unseemly sarcasm.

I ask him right off the bat, "I believe you went
to see Abbas before he left?"

"Right."

"It's not farfetched to suggest that you said
things that made him leave."

"He felt trapped, so he skipped out."

His insolence brings tears of fury to my eyes.

"Don't you know the meaning of mercy?" screams Umm Hany. "What's all this talk that's been going around? I watched Tahiya dying; I saw Abbas crazy with grief!"

Her words astonish me, and I want to know if the talk that's being spread around fits with what she saw.

"There's nothing to it!"

"He wouldn't kill her before your very eyes, you idiot," says Tariq.

"To suggest Abbas is a murderer is lunacy."

"His confession is being played out on the stage night after night."

"Thanks to him you've become an actor that audiences applaud even more than Ismail," says Umm Hany.

"Thanks to his crime—the crime that made him run away."

"He's staying in a quiet place," I say stubbornly, "to finish his new play."

"His new play! Don't fool yourself, Umm Abbas!"

Ah—in those days he was reasonable and obliging in spite of everything.

"What do you think, Halima? Tariq Ramadan wants to rent a room from us."

I objected. "No. No. Let him stay where he is."

"He's had a row with Umm Hany and has to leave her place. He's wandering around with no place to go, and things get more expensive every day."

"It won't be very pleasant having a stranger in the house."

"He needs us. And we need the money."

"He's no better than a tramp."

"He'd hoped we'd be kindhearted, especially you. We've got enough empty rooms to house an army."

Grudgingly I gave my consent. I had no use for him at all—a no-good actor living off the sweat of women. But I never imagined he'd do what he did to us.

Umm Hany pays us a surprise visit in the shop the day after I visited her. She evidently wants to apologize for the rude way her man had treated me. Like Tariq, she's in her fifties, but she's still buxom, not bad-looking, and has money.

"They're all talking about the success of the play," she remarks. "It's the biggest hit the theater's ever had."

"But the playwright doesn't want to show himself," I say sadly.

"He'll show up when he finishes his new play." The woman is silent for a while, then says, "What's being said is really absurd. But then Tariq is crazy!"

"Wouldn't it have been better for him to kill his mother?" Karam says sarcastically.

I have always had a liking for Umm Hany, and

the fact that she is related to my husband hasn't lessened my affection for her.

The house in al-Tambakshiyya, crowded with people, smelling of rubber, as though it were a bus. My aunt cleared a corner to receive Amm Ahmad Burgal.

"Don't forget the provisions, because next to God it's them we depend on."

"I came for something more important than that!" he said, more serious than usual.

"Open the bag, you snake charmer."

"It's about Halima."

My aunt looked at him and then at me, while the blood mounted in my cheeks.

"What! A husband?"

"That just about sums it up."

She looked at him inquiringly and he said, "Karam Younis."

"And who's Karam Younis?" asked my aunt.

"He's the company prompter."

"What does that mean?"

"He's a respectable employee of the theater."

"Do you think he's suitable, Amm Ahmad?"

"Yes, I do. But the important thing is what the bride thinks."

"The bride is a real beauty, as you know. But we are poor, Amm Ahmad."

It was my turn to speak. I'd been absolutely shattered by the bloody secret I was harboring; I didn't love the bridegroom, but I had no aversion toward him—a presentable young man. Perhaps he'd give me peace of mind, even happiness. Beleaguered by my aunt's stare, I mumbled, "I don't know anything about him worth mentioning."

"He has a job, he owns a house, and has a good reputation."

"By the goodness of God!" cried my aunt. Although she loved me, she'd be glad to be rid of me. As for me, I wanted to escape from that overcrowded house; and since Sirhan al-Hilaly was so rotten, there was no hope for me in that direction.

Life was unbearable, and hunger was knocking at the door.

"I've found the way to shut you up," he said, eyeing me disdainfully.

"Have you finally been cured of that hell of a drug?"

"Al-Hilaly has agreed to hold their soirees in our old house!" I didn't grasp his meaning, so he added, "We'll prepare a room for them to play cards in, and then we'll be on easy street."

"A gambling den?" I said, dismayed.

"You always describe things in the worst way. What would it be except a gathering of friends?" I protested, but he interrupted: "Don't you want a good life?"

"Yes, and a clean one, too!"

"If it's good, it will be clean. The only unclean thing is hypocrisy."

"And there's Abbas to think about," I murmured uneasily.

"I own this house, not Abbas. Your son is crazy. But surely you care whether he has enough to eat and clothes to wear!" he shouted.

The sun is hidden so often this autumn that I am grounded in melancholy. This narrow street sees at least one funeral going to Sidi al-Sharany every day. Whenever the man is not occupied with customers he starts talking to himself. I daydream of the things Abbas will do for me, but he has nothing to dream about.

Why don't we keep track of the happy moments, so that afterward we will believe them? Is he the same man? Was he really sincere? Is he the one who said, "I am indebted to Amm Ahmad Burgal for a joy that is almost more than a man can bear?"

I moved my head coquettishly. "Don't exaggerate!"

"Halima, who can be happier than a man whose heart has not beaten in vain?" He said it in a tone of voice that has vanished forever. Although I didn't love him, I loved his words, and their fervor warmed me.

* * *

On the appointed day waves of joy and fear roll over me. I go to the Indian bath, Umm Hany supplies me with a dress, a coat, and a pair of shoes, and I return from the hairdresser with a glorious halo, newly created from hair that had been neglected for a long time. The man looks at me disdainfully. "So you still have that weakness for playing the whore. Why don't you exploit it—in these illustriously dissolute days?"

I am determined at any cost not to ruffle the serenity of the evening. We go to the theater, where we are received with the respect we deserve. Sirhan al-Hilaly fixes me with an admiring stare.

"How is it that I don't see the playwright?" I say.

"He hasn't come, but I've told you enough about it."

My first hopes are shattered; and the internal radiance I'd been building up all day through a sense of renewed youth is extinguished. We go to see Amm Ahmad, who gives us tea and a sandwich as he always did. "It's like the old days," he remarks, laughing.

What are you talking about, Amm Ahmad? I wish it had never been. Even the one comforting result of it is absent. This place sets my nerves on edge and intensifies my sadness. At the proper time, though, we enter the theater and I am suddenly delighted to find it packed. "It's a success!"

I don't listen to his replies. The curtain is being raised on the old house. Events unfold one after another, and my agonies come to life before my eyes; now nothing is left of them except the memory of heaving sighs. Once more I find myself in hell. I condemn myself more than I ever have before. *That's when I should have left him, I say to myself, that's when I should have refused.* I am no longer the victim I thought I was.

But what is all this new damnation, this flood of crimes that nobody was aware of, this strange way I am being portrayed. Is it what he really thinks of me? What is this, son? You misunderstand your mother more than your father does and are even more unjust. Did I object to your marrying Tahiya out of jealousy and selfishness? What jealousy, what selfishness! No, no. This is hell itself. You almost make your father my victim. He was never the victim of anything except his mother. Do you see me as a prostitute, a madam? Do you think I'm the pimp who drove your wife to the tourist, greedy for his money? Is this a fantasy or is it hell? You are killing me, Abbas. You have made me the villain of your play. And the people are clapping—they're clapping!

The life has been knocked out of me. We're invited to the party in the cafeteria. "Shall we join them or leave?" the man asks. Feeling that he is trying to provoke and ridicule me, I challenge back: "Why shouldn't we join the party?"

But in spirit I cannot. I'm in a burning stupor; my head resounds with brawling voices as strange faces undulate before my eyes, shouting and laughing for no apparent reason. *My head is going to burst. The end of the world is approaching. Let the day of judgment come. I'll never obtain a fair judgment except before God. You murdered and betrayed and committed suicide! When will I see you? Will I ever see you again?*

We reach the old house at dawn. Throwing myself on the couch in the hall while he lights the heater, I hear him ask, "Did you like the play?"

"The audience liked it," I say lukewarmly.

"And the subject?"

"It's a powerful plot."

"Weren't we depicted as we really are?"

"Don't start thinking like that spiteful Tariq Ramadan."

"It's even more true than the real facts."

"There's no connection between the way I appear in that play and the real facts," I retort angrily. He lets off a repulsive laugh, while I suppress my anguish. "It's just a fantasy!" I say.

"All of them just as we know them in real life."

"It's largely imagination and very little actual fact."

"Then why did he portray you as he did?"

"That's his business."

"I thought that he loved and respected you."

"There's no doubt about that."

"You give yourself away with that bitchy look of yours."

"I know I'm right."

"Even Tariq! I never imagined you'd sink to such depths."

"Spare me your filthy thoughts!" I shout.

"That's the boy who threw us into prison."

"He wasn't describing himself, he was describing you!"

"How virtuous he made himself out to be!"

Fighting down my despair, I burst out, "When he comes back I'm going to leave this damn house and live with him!" and rush to my room. Behind the closed door my own tears strike me dumb. *How is it you don't understand your mother, Abbas?*

He came reeling, tumbling down the stairs, almost collapsing from fatigue and drunkenness. Then he spotted me. "Some eau de cologne!" he shouted. "I've had it!"

I went into my room to get the eau de cologne for him, and he followed me.

"Here you are."

"Thanks. I drank more than I should have."

"And you've had bad luck from the beginning of the evening."

After a while, he pulled himself together, looked

up at me, then went to the door and bolted it. I prepared to resist.

"Halima, you're magnificent!" he said.

"Let's go back upstairs." He came close to me and I drew back scowling.

"Are you going to be faithful to that lout?"

"I'm a respectable woman and a mother."

I made a rush for the door and got it open. For a moment he hung back, then he stepped outside and left the house.

All of them tried to seduce me, but I refused them. A whore?! It's true that I was raped once: and that I slept with your father, though not for long, before I turned celibate. I am a nun, my son, not a whore. Was it your father who painted this false picture for you? Desolate woman that I am, with wretched luck—I have no other hope but you. How could you picture me like that? I'll tell you everything! But when are you going to come back?

At night those carousers would slink into our old house, their shamelessness polluting the street that led to Sidi al-Sharany. My heart sank as I read their debauched looks and I worried about Abbas in his room. *But you are a jewel, son. You must not be stifled in the mire of poverty.* I'd put on a cheerful front as a welcome mat and take them to the room on the upper floor that we'd furnished with borrowed money. I was supposed to be the barmaid and serve them food and drinks; little did I understand that

we were at the beginning of a slippery path down-
ward.

"Don't be alarmed, dear. They're your father's
friends. All men do that."

"But, Mother, what have you got to do with it?"

"They're my colleagues from the theater and it
wouldn't be right for me to neglect them."

"A good, safe place," Sirhan al-Hilaly said,
beaming as he took his seat at the table, where
Ismail was shuffling the cards.

"Tahiya isn't allowed to sit next to Tariq," Fuad
Shalaby said with a chuckle.

Karam stood behind the cashbox at the edge of
the table and there was a laughing remark from
Tariq: "A votive offering box, Mr. Karam Younis?"

"No voice should be raised above the sound of
battle!"*

Karam was dissolving some opium in black tea.
What a beginning that knew no end!

I have returned myself to my prison cell, just as
I have returned the clothes I wore to the theater to
their owner. He sits here, his face morose and
blank; sells peanuts and melon seeds and joins the
customers in complaining about the times. Almost
to myself, I murmur, "The play's a success, that's
one consolation."

"One can't judge before a week has passed."

---

* This was a sentence used during the wars with Israel, and it has a special
connotation.

"What counts is the audience, their excitement, the effect it has on them."

"I wonder how much al-Hilaly paid him for it."

"The first work always brings in the lowest price. Abbas doesn't care about money." He bursts into that boisterous laugh of his, for which I curse him with all my heart.

In the vastness of his throne room, the evil deity gazed upon us smiling, "Welcome, Halima. I suppose your son is offering us a new play?"

"That's right."

"The last one was worthless," he said, addressing Abbas.

"I always profit from your comments," replied Abbas.

"I'd like to encourage you, at least for your mother's sake."

As the weeks roll by, it becomes apparent how successful the play is. Never has there been such a sellout at the theater. And the weeks turn into months. When will the playwright appear? He can think what he likes and let me suffer—but where is he? "I should think the people at the theater might have heard by this time from our absent one," I remark, loudly enough so that he has to hear.

"The last time I went there was ten days ago."

Tired of defending myself against his tongue, I make no demands of him. He has trotted off to the theater from time to time, whereas I haven't ventured to go since the opening night. On the next morning he goes again. A warm day, with the sun shining, and my heart flutters with consuming hope.

I could imagine miracles and strange happenings, but never that Abbas would marry Tahiya. Now Abbas was going to leave and Tariq Ramadan would be staying. Where was heavenly justice?

"Abbas, she's at least ten years older than you! She has a certain reputation and a history. Don't you understand what that means?"

He smiled. "Unfortunately you don't understand what love is," he said smugly. Bitterness welled in my soul, bringing back my buried sadness. "We're going to start a new life," he added.

"No one can escape his past."

"In spite of everything Tahiya is virtuous."

I wasn't being fair, I had forgotten about myself, but I wanted him to have a better lot in life. That's all there was to it.

Tahiya visited me, looking subdued, but determined. "Don't stand in the way of my happiness," she entreated me.

"You are stealing innocence."

"I'll be a devoted wife to him."

"You!"

The sharpness of my voice made her turn pale with anger. "Every woman in the theater began with Sirhan al-Hilaly!" she retorted.

My heart shrank. So they all knew or inferred what they didn't know. It was as if she were threatening me! I detested her. But he would remain my son, in spite of everything.

Surely, the man is later than usual? The last beams of sunlight are just leaving the walls along this narrow street. What's keeping him? Has he at last discovered the hiding place and gone there straightway? Will they come home together? I can see his fine-featured face smiling as he apologizes. I will not believe that this torture can go on forever. The play may well have pointed out the sources of my weakness, but I've always kept my heart clean. Haven't I atoned, then, sufficiently for that weakness? Who could have imagined that this kind of life would become the lot of the beautiful, chaste Halima? My heart holds nothing now but tolerance and love. O God, I accept your judgment. I have such compassion in my heart that it even pities Karam in his misery. I'll even forgive his brutality to me. When he returns with my beloved absent one's arm tucked under his, I'll forgive him everything.

Elation floods my being, but the feeling diminishes with the passing of time. A customer remarks as he leaves with his package, "You're in another world. Umm Abbas."

From the mosque the call to evening prayer reaches my ears as darkness creeps over the short winter day. There must be a reason for his delay. He isn't worth all this anxious waiting. What's

keeping him? The candle splutters in the winter
wind; I stand up, not intending to sit down again.
My mood has altered; he has deceived me unmer-
cifully. My patience is worn out, and I'll have to go
and look for him.

The first person I meet at the theater door is
Fuad Shalaby, who approaches me with unaccus-
tomed tenderness, holding out his hands to me.

"I hope it's false news," he says.

"What news?" I say as my last glimmer of hope
disappears. The man doesn't seem to know what
to say, so he remains silent. "Is it about Abbas?"

He nods his head, saying nothing more, and I
lose consciousness.

When I come to, I find myself on the couch in
the cafeteria and Amm Ahmad is taking care of me.
Fuad Shalaby and Tariq Ramadan are also there.
Amm Ahmad breaks the news to me in a funereal
voice and ends by saying, "No one believes it."

Fuad Shalaby takes me home in his car. On the
way he wonders aloud, "If he's committed suicide,
where is his body?"

"Then why did he write the note?"

"That's his secret," he answers. "We'll find out
in good time."

But I know his secret as I know my own heart
and I know my luck; he has killed himself. Evil is
playing flute music for Abbas.

ABBAS KARAM YOUNIS

Loneliness and the old house were the two companions of my childhood. I knew it inside out: the big, arched portals, the door with its small hinged panes of red, blue, and brown stained glass, the reception-room window with its iron bars, the upstairs and downstairs rooms with their high ceilings and painted wooden rafters, their floors covered with Masarany tiles; the old, shabby couches, mattresses, mats, and carpets, the undaunted tribes of mice, cockroaches, and wall geckos, the roof, crisscrossed with clotheslines like streetcar and trolley-bus wires, overlooking other roofs that on summer evenings were crowded with women and children. I roamed around the house alone, my voice echoing from its corners as I repeated my lessons, recited a poem, did a part from some play, or sang. Looking down on the narrow street for what might have been hours at a time, following the flow of people, I'd yearn for a friend to play with. A boy would call to me, "Come on down!"

"The door is locked, and my father has the key!"

I got used to being alone night and day; I wasn't afraid of anything, not even evil spirits.

"The sons of Adam are the only devils there are," my father would say.

"Be an angel," my mother would hasten to add.

When I had nothing to do, I would amuse myself by chasing the mice, the geckos, or the cockroaches.

My mother told me once that when I was a baby she used to take me in a leather cot to the theater and set me on a bench in the ticket booth. "I often nursed you in the theater," she said. I don't remember those times, of course, but I do recall events from a stretch of time when I must have been four years old. I used to wander around the theater in front or backstage, where, among other things, I'd listen to the actors memorizing their parts. My ears were filled with lovely songs and speeches—and with wicked oaths and blasphemies giving me an education I'd never have acquired from my parents, who were always either sleeping or working. On the opening night of every new play I was there with my father, half the time bedazzled, the other half asleep. It was about that time that I was given my first picture book, called *Ibn al-Sultan and the Witch*, a present from Fuad Shalaby.

That was how I came to understand heroes and villains in plays. Neither of my parents had time to give me any guidance; my father took no interest in education in any case, while my mother was content to repeat her only piece of advice—"Be an angel"—explaining that to be an angel was to love good, not to harm other people, and to have a clean body and clean clothes. My real tutors were, first, the theater, then books, when their time came, and finally people who had no relation to my parents.

As soon as I started school I loved it: giving me so many companions, it rescued me from my loneliness. I had to be self-reliant, though, at every step. I'd wake up early in the morning, eat my cold breakfast of cheese and boiled eggs from a plate that had been covered with a napkin the night before, dress, and leave the house quietly so I wouldn't arouse my sleeping parents. I'd return in the afternoon to find them getting ready to leave for the theater. I'd stay alone doing my homework, then amuse myself with games or books, at first only looking at the pictures, then reading the printed words—I'll never forget the generosity of Amm Abdu, the secondhand bookseller, who crouched on the sidewalk beside Sidi al-Sharany Mosque—and finally, after a supper of cheese and halva, I'd go to bed.

So I never saw my parents except for a while before sunset, and even part of this brief period was lost as they got ready to go out. Perhaps because there was so little intimacy or attention given to me, I was all the more attached to them. I yearned for them. My mother's beauty, sweetness, and tenderness bewitched me and I was enthralled by a

vision of that angelic nature she urged me to ac-
quire. His gentle way of playing with me and his
hearty laughter likewise made my father seem
wonderful. He was full of jokes, full of fun, and the
limited time we had together was never spoiled by
instructions, threats, or warnings. There was only
an occasioned reminder. "Enjoy being alone," he
used to say. "You're the king of the castle. What
do you want more than that? The only son, inde-
pendent of everyone. That's what your father was
like, and you'll be even more wonderful."

"He's an angel," mother would hasten to add.
"Be an angel, dear."

"Did Grandfather and Grandmother leave you
alone, too?" I asked him once.

"Your grandfather?" he replied. "He left me before I ever knew him. And your grandmother—she
worked at home."

Mother glowered, and I sensed that these words
carried a secret meaning. "Your grandfather died
young and your grandmother joined him, so your
father was left alone," she explained.

"In this same house?"

"Yes."

"If these walls could speak, they would tell you
the most fantastic tales," Father said.

It was a lonely house, but a harmonious one. At
that time Father and Mother were an agreeable
couple, or so, as I saw them in the gathering twi-

light, they always appeared to me. They shared conversation, jokes, and a deep affection for me. My father had a tendency to express himself a little freely, but Mother would stop him with a warning look, which I noticed sometimes and wondered about. The moment of leave-taking was painful and I would await Thursday with dwindling patience, for that was the night I could go with them to see a play.

As my learning increased, enabling me to read more, I asked for more pocket money to buy books, until I had accumulated a library of second-hand children's books. "Aren't you satisfied with going to the theater every week?" Father asked.

But I wasn't satisfied. My dreams took me far away to new horizons. One day I went so far as to tell him that I wanted to write plays!

He guffawed. "Dream about being an actor! It's preferable and more profitable."

"I have an idea, too."

"Really?"

I went on to outline the story of *Faust*, which was the last thing I had seen in the theater. I'd added nothing new except that I made the hero a boy of my age.

"How did the boy triumph over the devil?" asked Mother.

"You beat the devil by using the same tricks he does!" answered Father.

"Keep your thoughts to yourself!" shouted Mother. "Can't you see that you're talking to an angel?"

From an early age I was saturated with the love of art and virtue. I used to make lengthy speeches about these things to myself, in my solitariness, and I also learned about them from my schoolmates, among whom I was pretty conspicuous. Most of them were mean little devils, to be sure: whenever the teacher got fed up with them he'd shout, "You whorehouse brats!" There was a select little group, however, who were known for their innocence and good behavior, and I gravitated to them. We formed a Morality Squad, to battle against obscene language, and used to strike up the anthems of the New Egyptian Revolution, in which we believed implicitly. When a few of us pledged ourselves to unprecedented bravery, military or political, I pledged myself to the theater, seeing it as a platform for heroism, too, and one that would suit me, with my weak eyesight, which had obliged me to wear prescription glasses while I was still at primary school. Whatever differences there may have been among us, we all dreamed of an ideal world in which we made ourselves its most exemplary citizens. Even defeat failed to shake our basic ideals. As long as the slogans did not change and the leader remained the same, what did defeat mean?

Mother's face had grown haggard, though, and she muttered words I could not understand while Father would shrug his shoulders, as if things didn't matter, then burst out singing the national anthem in a raucous, mocking voice: "My country, my country, I have shed my blood for you."

The theater was shut down for some days, and for the first time I was able to enjoy having my parents at home all day long. Father even took me with him to the coffeehouse on Sharia al-Gaysh, a new experience. Defeat that time was not without pleasant side effects, but they were short-lived.

Mother was pouring tea. "Abbas," she said, "we are going to have a stranger living with us!" I stared at her in disbelief. "He's a friend of your father's. You know him, too. It's Tariq Ramadan."

"The actor?"

"Yes, he had to leave the place where he was living, and what with the housing shortage he hasn't been able to find a good place to go."

"He's a rotten actor. He doesn't look nice."

"People should help each other. And you're an angel, my dear."

"He'll come at dawn," said father, "and sleep until the afternoon. So except for his room, the house will still be your own special domain."

I was never aware of his arrival, but he usually left with my parents or immediately after them. He was insolent-looking and rough-spoken. He took a sham interest in me to flatter my parents, but I had no respect for him. One day, having spotted my library from where he was sitting in the hall, he asked me, "Schoolbooks?"

"Literary books and plays," Mother answered proudly. "You're speaking to a playwright!"

"Damn the theater! I wish I were a junk peddler. Or a hawker of meat from animal heads."

At that I asked, "Why do you only play small parts?"

He coughed abruptly. "My fate! I'm stalked by such crippling luck that if it weren't for your father's decency I'd have to sleep in public toilets."

"Don't scare the professor with such talk, Tariq," cautioned Mother.

He laughed. "A playwright must learn about everything, the good and the bad. Especially the bad. The theater has its fountainhead in wickedness."

"But good always triumphs," I declared with naive fervor.

"That's the way it is—in the theater!" he answered.

Like the coming of night, a vague change crept over them. Their silence wasn't the same silence, their talk wasn't the same, Father wasn't the same, nor was Mother. Our household had not been by any means without its minor differences or petty bickerings, but in general our life together had flowed along quite congenially. What, then, was the dark mystery that had slipped in between them? Her radiance had vanished; and he, who had always been an extrovert, laughing boisterously, making fun of everything and treating everyone amiably, had now become withdrawn. My mother's attachment to me—though still full of the same old tenderness—was tinged with a kind of grief which she could not succeed in hiding, while Father neglected me completely. An anxious dread of something unpleasant and unknown penetrated my soul.

At teatime one day, before they left, I heard Tariq advising them "not to give in to the devil."

"There is no devil except you," Mother answered bitterly.

"I'm not an adolescent," protested Father.

In deference to my presence, I surmised, Mother said nothing more. After they left the house I was struck with a sense of sadness and loss.

It was painfully clear that something had happened. I asked Mother about it, but she evaded the question, pretending nothing was wrong. When she and Father were alone in the hall I would hear them arguing fiercely. I would cower behind the open door listening.

"There's still a chance to be cured."

"Keep out of my private affairs!"

"But what you're doing reflects on us. Don't you realize that?"

"I hate being preached at."

"Opium killed my aunt's husband."

"Which proves that it has its uses."

"Your whole personality has changed. You're unbearable!"

I was seized by fear. I knew what opium was. I had learned about it watching a play, *The Victims*, from which the scenes depicting those doomed addicts had haunted me. *Was Father to become one of them? Was my beloved father headed for ruin?*

Before Father and Tariq returned I found myself alone with Mother. I gazed at her sadly.

"What's the matter, Abbas?"

"I know all about it." My voice was trembling. "It's something dangerous. I haven't forgotten *The Victims*."

"How did you learn about it? No, son. It's not quite as you imagine."

Father arrived at this point, upset, revealing that he had heard me. "Mind your own business, boy!" he yelled.

"I'm afraid for you," I said.

He shouted, in a voice more terrifying than I'd ever heard before, "Shut up, or I'll bash your head in!"

In my eyes at that moment he was transformed into a beast. The happy dream I'd had for so long was shattered. I retreated to my room, there to conjure up the whole panorama of a play that began

with Tariq's eviction from the house and ended
with my father's rehabilitation—as a result of my
efforts, naturally. I told myself that good would still
triumph if he could only find someone to help him.

But conditions went from bad to worse. He became more withdrawn; the father I had known no
longer existed, and in his new personality he cut
himself off from us on every occasion except when
his anger was aroused for whatever reason. Then
he would rain down curses and insults on us. I began to be afraid of him and kept my distance.
Mother was miserable and didn't know what to do.
"My salary isn't enough for the household," she
told him once.

"So go butt your head against a wall!" he said.

We were certainly no longer living as we used
to, spending much less and eating very simply.
Food and money didn't interest me, but how was I
going to buy books? It is unfortunate that the life
of the soul cannot do without money. The most
terrible blow, however, was that I had lost my father. Where was the man he'd once been? The look
in my eyes seemed to anger him. "You're a poor
specimen, not fit for life," he'd tell me. Things between him and mother deteriorated to the extent
that they each went their own way and had separate rooms. Our home was disintegrating and we
were living as strangers under the same roof. My
mother's fate was hard for me to bear. In my mind

sprang a scene revolving around a fight between
Father and Tariq: Father kills Tariq and is arrested,
and as he's leaving he turns to me and says, "If I
had only listened to what you said," after which
the old house regains its purity. Later, of course, I
felt remorse for the cruelty of my imagination.

I asked Mother, "How do you manage to make
ends meet all by yourself?"

"I sell little things. Pay attention to your work.
You're the only hope we have left."

"My heart is with you."

"I realize that, son, but the time hasn't yet come
for you to bear our burdens. You must study, to
get a good job."

"My ambition is to become a playwright."

"A profession that won't guarantee you security."

"I scorn material possessions. You understand
my nature."

"You may hate materialism, Abbas, but don't try
to ignore it altogether."

"Good will triumph, Mother," I assured her fervently.

I was as addicted to my dreams as my father was
to his opium. I imagined changing everything
around me and shaping it anew: I swept the gravel
market, sprinkled the streets, and dried up the ever-
flowing sewers; I tore down old houses and replaced
them with towering apartment blocks; I smartened

up the policemen, improved the conduct of the students and teachers, condemned drugs and drink, and conjured food from the air.

One afternoon the two of them were sitting in the hall, Father plucking his mustache with a pair of tweezers, Tariq darning his socks.

"Don't be taken in by the destitution of the poor," Tariq was saying. "This country is full of rich people no one knows about."

"Al-Hilaly is mining gold," said Father.

"Don't talk to me about al-Hilaly and his gold. Talk about women—and the petrodollar glut!"

"This scheme appeals to me. But our hands are tied."

"Abu al-Ala* used to live on a diet of lentils," I piped up.

"Deliver these pearls of wisdom to your mother!" Father yelled at me.

I fell silent, telling myself that they were just a couple of savages.

There was Tahiya, standing right in front of me, so incredibly attractive with her captivating eyes that I looked at her in a daze, not believing what I was seeing.

During the period before exams I used to stay up late at night and sleep in the daytime. The door

* Abu al-Ala al-Maarry (973–1057), born near Aleppo, was a blind poet-philosopher who is said to have been a skeptic, freethinker, and materialist.

had opened while I was pacing up and down in the
hall studying, and Tahiya had come in, with Tariq
Ramadan close behind. Father and Mother had already gone to bed. I knew Tahiya. I'd often seen
her onstage, doing bit parts, like Tariq, and I stared
at her now in bewilderment.

"What's keeping you up at this late hour?" she
said, smiling.

"He's a striver. He stays up at night in the pursuit of learning, and next week he is going to take
the middle school exams."

"Good for you."

They went upstairs to Tariq's room. My head
spun; my blood boiled. Was he bringing her to his
room behind my parents' backs? Didn't she have a
house they could go to? Was our house being
brought down to the lowest depths? I couldn't concentrate. My head was aflame with all the unquench-
able desires of puberty. Temptation had launched
an attack, which, in my struggle for purity, I fought
off by sheer willpower: my whole being raged fu-
riously until at last sleep overcame me.

In the afternoon, when they were sitting in the
hall, I approached my parents, and at the sight of
me Father asked apprehensively, "What's the matter with you?"

"Something very strange! You'd never imagine!"
I burst out heatedly. "Tariq brought Tahiya to his
room last night!" His heavy eyes turned toward

me, fixing on me. He said nothing, so I assumed he didn't believe me. "I saw it with my own eyes!"

"What exactly do you want?" he asked me coldly.

"I wanted to let you know, so you can set him straight and make him understand ours is a respectable home. You must tell him to leave."

"Pay attention to your studies, and leave matters belonging to the house to its owner," he replied sharply.

"She's engaged to him," Mother explained, in a voice that was muffled and abject.

"But they aren't married yet!"

"He wants to die of starvation," Father said to Mother sarcastically, pointing in my direction.

"We have made ourselves poor," I remonstrated in a burst of anger.

He seized his glass of tea to throw it at me, but Mother jumped between us and took me to my room. Her eyes were threatening tears. "There's no use hoping for anything from him," I said, trying to comfort her. "Just don't have anything more to do with him. I wish we could go away together, but where could we go? Where would we find a place to live? And where would our money come from!"

I couldn't find an answer. The truth stood before me in all its naked ugliness: Mother's moral reserves had collapsed in the face of the circumstances created by my father's addiction, for which he was obviously responsible, but from which he was helpless to escape. But even apart from his addiction, it struck me at times that he was totally without principles. I despised him and I rejected him. He'd made a brothel out of our old home. But I was weak, too. All I could do was cry.

I passed my examinations, but my success didn't make me as happy as it should have. I couldn't rid myself of my sense of shame; sorrow had settled deep within me. During the long vacation I took refuge in the library, and there I wrote a play. I begged Father to show it to Sirhan al-Hilaly, but he only replied, "We're not a children's theater."

Mother volunteered to submit it to him. Two weeks later she brought it back, saying, "Don't expect your first play to be accepted. What you must do is try again."

I was upset, but I didn't despair. How could I despair when my only hope was the theater? One day I happened to meet Fuad Shalaby in the reading room. We shook hands, I reminded him who I was, and his cordiality gave me the courage to ask, "How can I write an acceptable play?"

"How old are you?" he inquired. "What grade are you in now?"

"I'll be in secondary school next year."

"Can't you wait until you finish your education?"

"I feel as if I can write now."

"No, you don't understand life yet."

"I have a pretty good idea what it's all about."

He smiled at me, "What is life, in your view?" he asked.

"It's the struggle of the soul against materialism."

"And what role does death play in this struggle?" he asked with a broadening grin.

"It's the soul's final victory," I answered confidently.

"If things were only that simple." He patted my shoulder. "You need a lot more experience. Find out what interests people and what arouses them. I'd strongly advise you to plunge into life, taste it to the full, and wait for at least another ten years."

His words made me retreat even further within myself. He imagined that I'd been sheltered from temptation! Perhaps he was ignorant of what was going on in our house. And ignorant as well of the struggle in an adolescent soul, the unabating conflict of lust and loftiness, the battle in the mind between the erotics of Omar Khayyam and the epic romance of Magnun Layla, divided by the same contrast as between Tahiya, the wanton in the room upstairs, and the vision of her that haunted the imagination, or as between dirt strewn on the ground and banks of white clouds floating in the sky.

Strange things were going on in the room next

to Tariq's. The old furniture had been sold, replaced by beautiful new things bought at a public auction. A table covered with green baize stood in the center on a large carpet that had been laid over the Masarany tiles, and against the middle wall was a buffet. These were mysterious preparations. When I asked Mother she said, "Your father is getting it ready to spend his evenings there with friends and colleagues, as all men do." I stared at her suspiciously, the very mention of Father filling me with misgiving. "They'll spend the rest of the night here after the theater closes," she added.

I got into the habit of crouching in my room in the dark so that I could see things.

The truth of what was going on in our house could only be seen at night. These friends used to arrive very late. I would watch them come dribbling in—first Father, then al-Hilaly, Ismail, Salim al-Agrudy, Fuad Shalaby, Tariq, and Tahiya—then I'd sneak up to the top floor in the darkness. They would be seated around the table and the cards would already have been dealt.

It was gambling, just as I had seen it in the theater. The dramas of the stage, with their heroes and victims, had moved into our house, with the difference that these people, who contested with each other on the stage, here stood solidly together all on the side of evil. They were all actors, even the critic, and nothing was sure except lies. If the Deluge came again and if good intentions are worth anything, only Mother and I would deserve a place in a lifeboat. These changes were not our doing. But even Mother went so far as to prepare the food and drink. "You shouldn't have to serve these riffraff," I protested.

"They are colleagues, and I am the mistress of the house," she said by way of excuse.

"What house? It's nothing but a whorehouse, a gambling den."

"I'd like to get away from it, if we could only leave together. But what can we do?"

"This is why I hate money," I said, exasperated.

"But we can't get along without it. That's the tragedy. In any case, you are my only hope."

What is goodness? What is it without action? I had no energy for anything but daydreams, imagination, the domain of the theater. The house was infested with obscenity, and youth was no excuse for accepting the situation, but my hands were tied. I had no other recourse. The lives my schoolmates lived I could share only in the fire of my imagination, where beautiful words became images, not deeds, a Danse Macabre that I could only applaud from the edge of the ballroom floor.

Then Fuad Shalaby began bringing Doria, so that they could whisper together in the third room under the framed Bismallah* that had been a gift

* The first verse of the Fatha, Sura I, Koran.

from my grandfather. "Shalaby and Doria, too," I said to Mother. "We must leave."

"Not before you're able to," she replied, her eyes red.

"I'm suffocating."

"So am I, son, and more so."

"Is only opium responsible for all this?" She didn't answer. "Perhaps this opium itself is the result of something else. Perhaps it's not the real reason."

"Your father is mad," she sighed. "But it's my fault that I let him mislead me."

"I'd like to kill him."

She patted my arm. "Lose yourself in your studies," she whispered. "You are the only hope I have left."

The night that burned away my last illusion: through the doorway of my room I made out Sirhan al-Hilaly staggering downstairs in the dark, his hair disheveled, his eyes dull, driven by what looked like a kind of blind madness. I wondered why he'd fled so enraged from the battlefield of the card room. Mother came out of her room—I'd thought she was upstairs—to see what was happening, and met him below the last step. They whispered something I could not catch. She went into her room, and he slipped in after her. I jumped up, impetuously, but then stood stock-still, sensing that it was more important to me to learn the truth than to try to stop her. *My mother, too?* It is possible that for a few minutes I even lost consciousness. This was the blow that would leave my world in scorched ruins, echoing with the jeers of demons. I darted into the hall, then into her room, drowned in darkness, where I switched on the light. It was empty. I turned the light off again, backed into the hall, switched on the light there, and stood in a quandary. At that point my father came leaping down the stairs to confront me.

"What woke you up at this hour?" he said brusquely.

"I couldn't sleep," I answered, not knowing what I was saying.

"Have you seen Sirhan al-Hilaly?"

"He left the house."

"When?"

"A while ago. I don't know exactly when."

I returned to my room and stood there, in the dark, my head burning with insane thoughts, oblivious to the passing of time until the sound of footsteps brought me to my senses. People were leaving. Then no one was left in the hall except Mother and Father. I put my ear to the keyhole to hear what they were saying. "What went on behind my back?" I heard him asking her. She didn't answer, so he asked her another question. "Did Abbas see?" Again no answer. "He's the one who gave you the job. It's common knowledge that al-Hilaly hasn't spared anyone, not even Umm Hany." I didn't hear a sound from her, and he went on: "Everything has its price, that's what concerns me. As for you, though, you aren't worth being jealous over."

At last she spoke. "You're the lowest kind of vermin."

"Except for one little worm."

This was the reality. This was my father and this was my mother. The flames consuming my world grew fiercer. *Sheathe your dagger, for even Caesar has been slain. Cyrano de Bergerac fought against ghosts.*

I disowned both my parents, the pimp and the whore—whom I now remember having seen once whispering together with Fuad Shalaby, when I hadn't thought anything of it, and another time with Tariq Ramadan, when I hadn't had any doubts or suspicions. *All of them, all, without any exception. Why not? She is my foremost enemy: Father is insane, an addict, but Mother is the engineer of all the evil in the world.*

My mother's voice, calling my name, reached me in my room. How strange that my hatred of Father had taken a definite form, while my feelings toward her expressed themselves not in simple aversion, but in a confused tumult of resentment.

She hurried in and took me by the hand. "Leave your reading for a while—it's not often we have the chance to sit together and talk."

She took me into the hall, sat me down beside her, and served me tea. "I'm not pleased with you these days," I remarked.

"I understand what's grieving you," she said, "but don't make my suffering worse." I avoided looking at her. "The time of deliverance is drawing closer and we'll leave together."

What an imposter she is! "This house can only be purged by fire," I muttered.

"Isn't it enough that my heart worships you!" *Shall I dump the ashes of my burned-out heart? Shall I bury her?* But my fantasies had so destroyed every response within me that I could only stand bewildered before her gaze. "Are you writing another play?" she asked.

"Yes. It will remind you of the play called *The Drunken Woman*," I said, referring to the one that dealt with the dark world of fallen women.

"Oh no," she said, "in your plays, son, you should let the light in your heart shine forth."

At that moment Father came out of his room, and Tariq and Tahiya came down. I got up to go back to my room, but Tahiya wouldn't let me pass. "Sit with us for a while, author," she said gaily.

It was probably the first time she had paid any

attention to me, so I sat down. Tariq laughed. "He's going to be the author of a tragedy," he remarked.

"He's sick with the disease of virtue!" my father muttered.

Tahiya took a sip from her glass. "How beautiful," she murmured, "that anyone could be virtuous in these days."

"As you can see, his eyes are weak," said Father, "so he can't see what's going on around him."

"Leave him in his heaven," replied Tahiya. "I'm also a lover of virtue."

"Your virtue is the kind that puts everyone in a good humor," said Tariq, chuckling.

"He has his mother's good looks. He's strong like his father. He should be a Don Juan," said Tahiya, sipping her tea.

"Just look at his glasses!" scoffed Father. "His trouble is he can't see."

They went out, leaving me furious and full of rebellion. In my imagination I eagerly set about tearing down and rebuilding.

When Tahiya stood in my way, however, she had brushed against me and set a new dream in motion. She was no better than my mother. What made her seem so much less objectionable? Later, alone, I recalled her touch, and a new idea for a play sprang from the inferno inside me: it revolved around this old dwelling my grandfather had built by the sweat of his brow, and how it had become a whorehouse. This was the central conception. The only inkling I had that it might be a success was the trembling joy that permeated my being. *Would such a plot serve as the basis of an effective play? Could there be a play without love?*

A faint knock at my door. I answered it and found Tahiya dressed to go out. *What had brought her here before teatime?* With one remark—"Everyone's asleep except you"—she walked in and stood in the middle of the room. Her eyes took in everything. "A bed. A desk," she noted. "This is a home, not just a room. Have you got any sweets here?"

I apologized for having none.

Her ripe body spread an aura outward from the middle of my room, exuded allure. For the first time I noticed the translucence of her eyes, the color of honey.

"I guess I should leave, since you have nothing here except books." But instead of turning to go, she said, "You're probably wondering why I'm ready to leave so early. I'm going to my apartment in Sharia al-Gaysh. Do you know it? It's one streetcar stop from Bab al-Shariya. Building 117."

Her feminine fragrance had already intoxicated me. "Wait!" I exclaimed. "I'll get you some sweets."

"I'll find what I want in the street. You're very nice."

For an instant, because of her presence, I forgot the struggle that had raged in my conscience. "You're the one who is really nice," I answered.

She gazed at me with a look that inspired dreams, then moved languidly toward the door. In spite of myself, I murmured, "Don't leave. I mean, there's no hurry."

She gave me a winning smile, said, "Until we meet," and went away, leaving behind her, in that tranquil room, a storm of the most delightful excitement. *Why would she come without pretext, and why would she mention the number of her apartment so casually?* How my deprived, obstinate, and naive heart throbbed. For the first time it had discovered a real woman to take an interest in, rather than Layla, Lubna, Mayya,* Ophelia, or Desdemona.

Over the next few days every furtive glance we exchanged was imbued with a new meaning that confirmed our fascination with each other. Heedless of those present, we would converse warmly. I asked myself, with puzzled persistency, whether I was being transported upward or pushed down to the depths.

In spite of the Amsheer† wind howling outside, the shouting and the ruckus reached me from the

---

*Female characters in well-known Arab love lyrics.
†Coptic name of the windy month that follows Touba, the coldest month, corresponding to January. The rich weather lore associated with the Coptic calendar has kept it in use throughout Egypt by both Copts and Muslims.

upper floor. I leaped up the stairs to investigate and saw Tariq slapping Tahiya's face in the hall. Astonishment froze me in my tracks. She retreated into their room.

"Did we disturb you?" Tariq said coolly.

"Excuse me," I spluttered, suppressing my agitation.

"Don't be upset. This is part of our daily routine. Enjoy it."

"This time I'm not going to come back!" said her trembling voice, raised almost to a shout, from inside the room.

Tariq went in, closing the door behind him, and I went back down, a new sadness plunging me deeper into despair. *Why would a beautiful woman like Tahiya put up with a life of abuse from a man like Tariq? Does love give light only so as to reveal tragedy?*

For two days she stayed away, but on the third she came back, her face glowing. My heart contracted and my grief grew greater still. I despised her conduct, but my love for her now was so obvious that it could not be ignored. It had probably come into being, taken root, and continued growing for a long time without my being aware. That day as they were leaving she stopped to straighten her stockings and let fall a small piece of folded paper before catching up with the others. I opened out the paper, my heart trembling with joy, and read the address and the time.

* * *

There were only two rooms, with a small entrance hall, but her flat was attractive, clean, and redolent of sweet incense. A round orange vase on the table in the hall held a bouquet of roses. She received me wearing a dark blue dress. Pointing to the flowers, she said, "To celebrate the day of our meeting." Pent-up desire drove me into her arms. We embraced for a long time, and if the choice had been mine, the encounter would have been finalized before we separated, while I was still tasting the delight of my first kiss. But she freed herself gently from my arms and led me into the blue sitting room, simple but tidy, where we sat down side by side on the large sofa. "It's daring of us," she breathed in a low voice, "but it is the right thing to do."

"The right thing!" I repeated emphatically.

"We can't possibly hide what's between us any longer."

"The right thing," I said, determined to do away with childishness. "I have loved you for a long time."

"Really! I've loved you, too. Can you believe that I am in love for the first time!" Incredulous, I said nothing. "You've seen for yourself," she said earnestly, "and possibly heard more. It's been groping around, not love."

"A life unsuitable for someone like you," I said sadly.

"A beggar can't choose what's suitable and what isn't," she said.

"Everything has got to change."

"What do you mean?"

"We must begin a proper life."

"I've never met anyone like you before," she said with fervor. "They were all beasts."

"All of them?" I protested.

"I don't want to hide anything from you: Sirhan al-Hilaly, Salim al-Agrudy, and finally Tariq." I was speechless, my thoughts turning to my mother. "If you're the kind of person who can't forget the past," she went on, "there's still time to change your mind."

I took her hand in mine, possessed by a strong inner drive to meet the challenge. "The only thing that concerns me is true worth," I assured her.

"My heart always told me that you were bigger than any of my petty fears."

"I'm not a child."

"But you're still a student," she said, smiling.

"That's true; I still have a long stretch ahead of me."

"I have a little bit saved up," she said simply. "I can wait."

But I had been captivated not only by love but

also by longing to escape from that sullied, joyless house. I therefore decided to take a step that would irrevocably open a new path.

"On the contrary," I said quietly, "we must get married right away."

She blushed, looking all the more beautiful, but seemed too shaken to speak.

"That's what we have to do," I repeated.

"I want to change my way of life!" she said, full of sudden excitement. "I want to get away from the theater, too. But are you sure your father will still support you?"

"He certainly won't do that." I smiled sadly. "And I'm certainly not going to accept his filthy money."

"How in the world are we going to get married then?"

"I'll be finished with secondary school quite soon and I won't be drafted, because of my eyesight. There's no reason why I shouldn't get a job. My talents depend on individual study, not on taking courses."

"Will your earnings be enough?"

"My father has asked to be relieved of his work in the theater. He can live easily on what he earns from gambling and other sources and he's been looking for someone to take his place as prompter. I'll apply for the job. At least I'll be in the theater, in the kind of world where I belong. And since you hold a lease on this flat, we won't have the problem of finding somewhere to live."

"Shall I go on working in the theater until our circumstances improve?"

"No!" I said sharply. "You must keep away from those men."

"I have a little put by, as I said, but it won't last until you can stand on your own feet."

"We'll just have to make do," I said fervently, "until we achieve our goal."

At that point we surrendered to passion and forgot everything for a while, not saying a word until she freed herself tenderly from my arms and whispered, "I have to get away from Tariq. I'm not going to see him again."

"He'll come here," I said. The very mention of his name upset me.

"I won't open the door to him."

"I'll tell him everything," I declared.

"Abbas," she said uneasily, "please don't let things get out of hand."

"I'm not afraid of facing him," I boasted.

I returned to Bab al-Shariya a new being. For the first time I had seen her through the eyes of a lover saying goodbye, and she appeared even lovelier and more worthy of sympathy. *I'll be moving soon*, I said to myself, *out of the audience to play a role on the stage of life, out of the putrid atmosphere of the old house to breathe a purer and newer air.*

I sat waiting in the empty hall until I saw Tariq coming downstairs. He greeted me and asked, "Hasn't Tahiya arrived?"

"No," I answered, jumping up to confront him.

"I didn't run across her at the theater."

"She's not going to the theater."

"What do you mean?"

"She's not coming here, and she's not going to the theater."

"Where did you discover all these secrets?"

"We're going to be married."

"What?!"

"We've agreed to get married."

"You son of a . . . ! Are you crazy? What did you say?"

"We decided to treat you honorably."

He took me by surprise, hitting me hard enough to make me angry. I punched him back and nearly floored him. All of a sudden, there were my parents, rushing blindly toward me.

"It's ludicrous!" Tariq yelled. "Mama's boy is going to marry Tahiya!"

"Tahiya!" Mother cried. "What kind of lunacy is this? She's ten years older than you!"

Tariq began to threaten us, so Mother told him to take his belongings and get out.

"I'll stay here until Doomsday," he shouted as he left.

For a while, no one spoke. Then Father muttered

the words of an old song—"In love, you whom I
mourned for"—tingeing them with scorn.

"Abbas," Mother said, "this is just a rash in-
fatuation."

"No, it isn't! It's a new life."

"What about your dreams, your future?"

"I will attain them in the most praiseworthy way
possible."

"What do you know about her?"

"She told me frankly about everything."

"A child of the theater," Father sneered, "who
knows all the tricks. And you're a strange boy!
Your knowledge of your mother should have made
you forswear the female species."

At that my mother took me to my room. "She
has a certain reputation and a history," said
Mother. "Don't you understand what that means?"

I avoided looking at her, the old pain stabbing
again. "Unfortunately you don't understand what
love is," I retorted. "We're going to start a new
life."

"No one can escape his past!"

Alas, she was unaware of what I knew about
hers. "In spite of all that," I asserted, "Tahiya is
virtuous."

I wish I could say the same about you, Mother.

No sooner had I completed secondary school
than I went to see Sirhan al-Hilaly about taking
over my father's job. Tahiya and I got married at

once, and I bade farewell to the old house and its inhabitants without any ceremony, just as if I were going off to school or to the library. Father didn't utter a word of congratulation or wish us well. "What made you put so much effort into your schoolwork," he said, "if all it amounts to is a prompter's job?"

Mother, however, hugged me and burst into tears. "May the Lord help you and protect you from evil people," she said. "Go in peace, and don't forget to visit us."

But I had no intention of ever coming back to hell. I was eager to lead a different life, to breathe pure air, and to forget the abyss I'd been mired in, the pain I'd suffered.

Tahiya was waiting for me and so was love. With her I found all the happiness that can arise from the union of two harmonious people. She was bewitching, whether talking or silent, serious or having fun, even cooking or cleaning. What my salary could not cover, she made up from her savings. The sense of peace I gained from her replaced all my earlier unrest, disorientation, grief, and suppressed anger. I would come home about three in the morning, wake up around ten, and after that there was ample time for both love and writing.

We pinned our hopes together on my expected success as a playwright. Until that success came, we were willing to live simply, even frugally, doubling our efforts, patience, and hopes because of the joy we shared. Tahiya proved her strength of will in a fitting way by not touching a drop of wine, thus breaking a long-standing habit. To save money, she even stopped smoking. She confessed that she would once have sunk to opium smoking if it hadn't made her sick and given her a permanent aversion. She was such a proficient housewife that one time I remarked, "Your house is always clean and tidy, your food is delicious, and you have good manners. You shouldn't have had to . . ."

"My father died and my mother married a bailiff," she said, interrupting my train of thought. "She neglected me, and he mistreated me, so I had to run away."

She didn't elaborate, and I didn't ask her to. I nevertheless imagined what had happened to make her one of Sirhan al-Hilaly's actresses. And in spite of myself I recalled that my mother had worked in the same theater, likewise at his mercy. I was privately waging war, a campaign against all the kinds of enslavement to which people are exposed. *Would the theater be enough of a base for this war? Would my concept of the old house, which had sunk so low as to become a brothel, be a sufficiently strong ally?*

Tahiya's gentleness and sweetness never failed; even in my happy childhood, my parents' relationship had never been like that. She was an angel, the proof of which was her determination to cast

aside the way of life that had tainted her sad past.
And she truly loved me as was clear from her desire
to have a child. I didn't want that to happen, however, being afraid, with our limited income, that it
would interfere with my life as an artist, which was
dearer to me than anything else in the world, dearer
even than love, though I hated to disappoint her,
and my own ethics forbade me to give in to selfishness.

At exactly the time when the cost of living had
soared beyond both our expectations and our
means, and we found ourselves forced to think of
different ways of surviving, Tahiya's hope of being
pregnant was fulfilled; and I was beset by a new
anxiety, obliged now to take into account both the
near and the distant future. Our state of affairs convinced me that there was no way out except to find
another job, if that were possible.

I'd heard that American and European writers
used typewriters instead of pens, so I'd learned to
type. On my way to the theater I used to pass by
a typing bureau called Faisal, and I applied there
for a job. The owner immediately accepted me on
his terms: I agreed to work from eight in the morning to two in the afternoon and to be paid by the
piece.

Tahiya received the news with mixed feelings.
"You're going to go to bed at three in the morning,

wake up at seven, at the latest, instead of ten, work from eight until two, then come home at three to get another two hours' sleep, at most, between four and six. You won't get any rest. You won't have time for reading or writing."

"What can I do?"

"Your father has lots of money."

"I'm not going to accept one filthy millieme," I said indignantly.

I refused to go on arguing. She was certainly an exceptional woman, but she was quite practical when it came to matters of living, preferring in the depths of her heart to ask my father for help rather than see me bury myself in work that would impinge on my time, my creativity, and my strength.

I took two days off from work at Faisal in order to finish my play, which I offered to Sirhan al-Hilaly. He looked at me smiling. "You haven't given up?" he asked.

During the days of waiting for his reaction I lived with my beautiful dreams. Art had become not only the one way I had of satisfying my deepest longings but also my only route to actual living. I'd begun writing this particular play, however, before I'd had the idea about the house as a brothel; it hadn't yet jelled, but I'd finished it anyway, still happy with its idealistic moral philosophy.

Sirhan al-Hilaly returned it to me with one remark: "You still have a long way to go."

"What does it lack?" I asked, sighing.

"It's a story," he said crisply, "but it won't do as drama." There was no encouragement for me to continue.

What unparalleled agony! Worse than what I'd gone through in the old house. Failure in art is death itself—that's the way we're made—and art, in my case, was not just art but the surrogate for the action that an idealist like me is unable to take. *What will I have done to combat the evil around me? What will I do if I have not the strength to carry on the struggle in the only field granted me, the theater?*

The days went by. I worked nonstop, like a machine, making hurried love, cutting myself off from the life of the spirit. No reading. No writing. Living—reduced to daily encounters with universal blight, the filth and slime of overflowing sewers, and a beastly transportation system—lost all its joy. Examined during brief intervals of relaxation, with Tahiya close to me, my life seemed a calendar of days dwindling away in sterile mockery. It was in such an oppressive atmosphere that we exchanged endearments, buoyed by cautious daydreams, the life that pulsated in her womb playing on the strings of my hoped-for, dreamed-of success— though sometimes the dreams burned with wild anger, against shame and sin, with visions of fire destroying the old house and the fornicators in it. I could never have such visions, however, without feeling ashamed and self-recriminatory afterward. It's quite true that my heart held not one speck of love for my father, but I had a sort of wavering compassion for my mother.

When I expressed this inner conflict, Tahiya said to me, "A secret gambling den is a crime in the eyes of the law, but the rise in prices is just as bad."

"Would you be willing to have that go on in your house?" I asked.

"God forbid! But what I want to say is that there are people who, when they are in trouble, act like a drowning man and grab at anything to save themselves."

I told myself that I was acting like that drowning person, even though I had committed no crime according to the law: to earn our bread, I had filled all my time with worthless work, and life in consequence had become a dry reed. Wasn't that somehow criminal, too?

The days passed by, my agony increased, and some satanic power enabled me to give form to my innermost desire: sitting at the typewriter, I was suddenly overcome with a longing for freedom, for my lost humanity, and for my dissipated creativity. How could the prisoner break his chains? I pictured a world, a righteous world, with no sin, no bonds, no social obligations; a world throbbing with creativity, innovation, and thought, nothing else; a world of dedicated solitude, without father, mother, wife, or child; a world where a man could travel lightly, immersed in art alone.

Ah! What a dream. What kind of devil lurks in the heart that has consecrated itself to goodness? The image of my angel brought me remorse. *I should feel mortally ashamed before that woman, who exudes love and patience. May God protect my wife and forgive my parents.*

"What are you thinking about?" she asked. "You're not listening to what I'm saying."

I touched her hand tenderly. "I'm thinking about the new arrival and what we should have ready for him."

One day, about to sit down at Amm Ahmad's bar, I noticed a morose look on his face that portended bad news. "Are you all right, Amm Ahmad?" I asked.

"It seems you haven't heard yet."

"I just arrived. What's happened?"

"The police," he began. "Last night—I mean at dawn—they made a raid on the house."

"My father's?" He nodded. "And what happened?"

"The same as always happens in such cases: they let the gamblers go free and arrested your parents."

I was absolutely devastated. Filled with a suffocating anxiety, I forgot my former sentiments, forgot my enduring anger. My father's and mother's dreadful fate stabbed me so deeply that I broke into sobs. Sirhan al-Hilaly summoned me at once. "I'll engage an expert lawyer as legal counsel for them," he told me. "The money has been confiscated. They came across quite a lot of drugs. There's some hope, though."

"I want to see them right away."

"No doubt you'll be able to, but I'm afraid I can't let you off work tonight. That's a matter of course in the theater. The show must go on, even when there's been a death. I mean, even the death of a loved one doesn't prevent a professional actor from playing his role. Even if it's a comic one."

I left his room feeling defeated, and the guilty memory of my frightful dreams intensified my suffering.

Taher was born just before the trial, into an atmosphere so heavy with dejection, so teeming with sorrows and humiliations that Tahiya hid even her joy in front of me. Before the baby was a month old his grandparents went to prison. He was sickly, which worried us both, but I fled, to drown my anxieties and sense of guilt in endless work. I was destined, however, to face another blow, so cruel that it would make me almost forget the sorrow I felt then.

When Taher was just over five months old, Tahiya's health broke down. We diagnosed the malady ourselves as influenza, but after a week had gone by with no signs of improvement, I fetched the local doctor. "She must have tests done," he said when we were alone. "I suspect typhoid." As a precautionary measure he prescribed some medicine and suggested moving her to a fever hospital.

Having made up my mind to look after her myself, I rejected the idea, though I had to quit my job at Faisal's typing bureau. To make up for the loss of income and to cope with added expenses, I sold the refrigerator. I became Tahiya's nurse and Taher's nursemaid, moving him into the other room and giving him his bottle while I tended her, applying myself to both tasks with devotion. Unlike the baby's, Tahiya's health improved.

Driven by love and a sense of grateful indebtedness to this woman who had always been so sweet and good to me, I did all I could for her. After three weeks of care she'd recovered enough strength to leave her bed and sit in a comfortable chair in the sunshine. She had lost most of her fresh beauty and all her vitality, but she asked incessantly about the baby. Her recovery gave me a little respite, despite Taher's continuing misery. He received no attention during my long hours at the theater, from eight in the evening until two in the morning, and I had hoped that Tahiya would soon be able to take over my duties. Suddenly, however, her condition deteriorated, so much so that I called the doctor again. "She shouldn't have got up," he said. "She's had a relapse. It often happens, with no serious results." I went back to my nursing feeling twice as depressed but with twice the determination. Umm Hany got to know about our predicament, and offered to stay with Tahiya during my absences.

Despite the assurance of the doctor's repeated visits, my heart contracted, and I had a sense of imminent sorrow. Was I going to have to go on living without Tahiya? Could I bear to live without her? Torn between her and the weakening baby, I worried about how quickly the money was running out and wondered what else I could sell. I would gaze at her sallow, shrunken face, summoning up recollections of our beautiful relationship, as if I were bidding her farewell. The whole world seemed black to me. When the final warning came, I was outside the flat, returning from the theater, had just rung the bell, and heard Umm Hany's loud wailing. I closed my eyes in acceptance of my fate, and opened my heart to the blackest sorrow.

A week after Tahiya's death Taher joined her, as was to be expected. The doctor had predicted it. I hadn't had a proper chance to learn what fatherhood was like: his tortured existence had always been a source of pain to me.

I don't remember anything about those days except Tariq Ramadan's weeping. Having cried my heart out alone, I had been able to bear up fairly well in front of the people gathered for the funeral, when all of a sudden Tariq's outburst made everyone from the theater turn to look at him. I wondered what lay behind this show of emotion. Had he loved her, this animal, who had moved his canned imitation of love to Umm Hany's house? I couldn't help speculating on the meaning of his tears, not only in my capacity as a widower but also as a dramatist; for not even in my dazed grief had I forgotten my dormant aspirations.

This was loneliness: a silent house filled with memories and ghosts, a heart ravaged not only by sorrow but also by a sense of sin, for the icy reality that stared me in the face also whispered in my ear that my imaginings had not been realized. I wanted to forget the imagination, even if it meant grieving more deeply.

Yet when grief is so intense, plunges so deeply that it finally hits bottom, it begins to radiate a strange intoxication, bringing a little solace with it. Could it be that Tariq Ramadan, when he affronted the mourners with an outburst of tears deep down inside, had been laughing? This, too, is loneliness: grief, accompanied by forbearance and challenge. Together they showed me a prospect that tempted me: lifelong bachelorhood, satisfied pride, and immersion in writing until death.

I had already begun drawing up plans for a play to be entitled *The Old House—The Brothel* when in a flash came a vision of Tahiya as she had been, strong and well, lusciously full of *joie de vivre*. A new idea sprang up: the setting would actually be the old house, its actual transformation into a brothel would still pertain, and the characters would be actual people themselves; but the plot would be what I'd imagined and not the actuality. Which—what I'd imagined or what had actually happened—was theatrically stronger? What I'd imagined, unquestionably. In reality the house had been raided by police and sickness had killed Tahiya and her son, but there was another murderer: my imagination, which had informed the police and had killed both Tahiya and the baby, and was thus the ultimate protagonist in a plot that fulfilled all the requirements of a drama—a plot through which I would confess, do penance, and write a real play for the first time. I would challenge Sirhan al-Hilaly to reject it, though he and a few others might think I was confessing to outward reality rather than to the substance of a dream. Inwardly, art is a means of expurgation, outwardly a means of battle, incumbent on men born and reared in sin and determined to rebel against it. Nothing else matters. The fever of creation had infected my whole being.

On my way to keep my appointment with Sirhan al-Hilaly, the month allotted to reading the play having now gone by, my heart had been beating wildly. A refusal this time would be beyond my endurance. It would finish me. The glee I saw hiding in his eyes made my heavy heart tremble, however, and I sat down where he indicated with increasing optimism, to hear his booming voice say, "At last you've created a real play," and to feel him staring at me interrogatively, as if to ask, "How did you do it?" At that moment all my cares momentarily evaporated and I could feel my face going red. "It's wonderful, terrifying, potentially a great success! Why did you call it *Afrah al-Qubbah?*"

"I don't know," I replied, bewildered.

"Artists' wiles are beyond me," he said with a resounding laugh. "I wonder if you're alluding to the joys—shall we say?—of moral struggle in the midst of spreading vermin? Or are you being ironic, the way we are when we call a black servant girl Sabah or Nur?"* I smiled in agreement. "I'll give you three hundred pounds," he said. "Generosity is, probably, my sole virtue. It's the largest sum ever paid for a first play." *If only you could have lived long enough to share my happiness.* "But don't you expect some embarrassing questions?" he asked, after a moment of reflection.

"It's a play. There's no need to look beyond it."

"Well answered. I'm not interested in anything but the play. It's bound to arouse a storm of suspicion, though, among people we know."

"I don't care if it does," I said calmly.

* Meaning *morning* and *light*.

"Bravo! What else have you got?"

"I hope to begin writing a new play soon."

"Good for you! It's the rainy season for you. I'm all anticipation. I'll spring it on the company as a surprise this coming fall."

My little flat made me subject to frequent fits of gloom and I wished I could find another place to live, but where? Changing the rooms around, selling the bed, buying a new one, I realized that Tahiya had penetrated much further into my life than I had ever imagined. My mourning was not the kind that began deep and became lighter. It had been comparatively bearable to begin with—probably because of the state of shock I'd been in—but then became so entrenched that I could only hope for forgetfulness through the passage of time. My apparent lack of reaction would look to many people like evidence that I had killed her. *But she knows the whole truth now.*

Shortly before the onset of autumn, my parents were released from jail. A sense of duty, which in my mind always overrides sentiment, led me to welcome them with sympathetic charity, but to see them so broken deepened my depression. I proposed to Sirhan al-Hilaly that they return to their former jobs in the theater; I would make work available for them, freeing myself from the job so as to spend all my time on my art. He agreed, but they absolutely refused, making it clear that they wanted to have nothing more to do with either the theater or its people, none of whom, with the exception of Amm Ahmad Burgal and Umm Hany, had even taken the trouble to visit them.

I was glad. Father now conformed to the picture I had drawn of him in the play. He was still strange, despite his forced withdrawal from opium; we had nothing in common, and I didn't understand him. But then I don't lay claim ever to have understood him with any certainty. It was the play that had willed me to present him as the victim of poverty and drugs. *I wonder what he'll say about his role. Will I be able to face him after its performance?*

As for Mother, she was still attached to me and still wanted to live with me, but I wanted to be unencumbered, to discover some new place to live on my own, even if it was only one room. If I didn't feel any love toward her, neither did I harbor any feelings of hate. *And she will be dismayed when she sees herself portrayed on the stage and realizes that I was aware of everything she had tried to hide from me.* After that, would I be able to look her in the eye? Never!

I would leave them to themselves, but in some security. The idea of the shop—Amm Ahmad Burgal had suggested it—was a good one. I hoped they would make a living, and sincerely repent.

I was face to face with Tariq Ramadan. We'd always exchanged the usual greetings in passing. This time, however, with typical insolence, he actually intruded into my solitude. Tariq is one of those few who have no notion at all of what it is to feel awkward or embarrassed over doing anything at other people's expense; I'd scolded Umm Hany several times for living with him.

"I came to congratulate you," he said, "on the play."

I didn't believe him. *You came, rather, to conduct a cruel inquiry.* I tried to be courteous, however, and thanked him.

"The hero is totally disgusting, an odious person," he said. "The audience won't have any sympathy for him." The remark was mainly his sly way of letting me know the director's opinion and I ignored this criticism completely: the hero wasn't like that, either in real life or in the play. I saw that Tariq was simply attacking me, nothing more or less, and I looked at him so contemptuously that he asked, "Didn't it occur to you that the events of the play would make people think the worst about you?"

"That doesn't matter to me."

"What a cold-blooded killer you are!" he blurted out, suddenly showing agitation.

"Now you're going back to the past," I said disdainfully. "As far as I'm concerned, the main thing was an attempt at love, whereas with you it was all nothing but an ordeal marked by your own spite."

"Are you going to be able to defend yourself?"

"I haven't been accused."

"You're going to find yourself in the office of the prosecuting attorney."

"You're a stupid ass."

He got up. "She deserved to be killed in any case," he said contemptuously. "But what you deserve," he added, "is hanging." Then he left.

This hateful visitation made me feel as if I were being caught up in a whirlpool; it convinced me that I had to hide myself somewhere, out of reach of these ignoramuses. *Did I really deserve to be hanged? Not in the least, not even if I were charged with my own hidden desires. My imaginings—symbols of escape from actual burdens, not of flight from love or my loved one—had arisen out of temporary agitation, not out of deep-seated feelings. Anyway, I could no longer go on living where this devil could get at me.*

An agent suggested a room in the pension La Côte d'Azur in Helwan.* This again was loneliness, but of a different kind: myself, my craft, and my imagination. Keeping mostly to my room, I set aside time during the night to get some exercise by walking. As I'd resigned from my job and had

---

*A town about twenty-five kilometers south of Cairo. With its warm, dry climate and mineral springs, it was once a famous spa.

nothing to do but write, I told myself that I had to sit down and choose one of the dozens of ideas floating around in my head, then concentrate. When it came to it, however, it became quite clear to me that after all I didn't possess a single idea. What was wrong?

I wasn't living merely alone, but in a vacuum. My grief for Tahiya returned, penetrating, deep, and subjugating. Even the image of Taher took shape before my eyes, innocent, emaciated, struggling against some unknown entity. In my attempt to escape from my depression by writing, I would encounter only a void. I was burned out. And what had extinguished the flame had not only smothered my creativity but left nothing in its place except endless listlessness and aversion to life itself.

Meanwhile, much to my bafflement, I read a great deal about the success of the play, dozens of critiques lavishing praise on the author and predicting how much the theater would profit from his talent. This critical reception, coming on the heels of my tortured attempts at writing in this hell of barrenness, this hell of sorrow and want, with my resources dwindling every day, was sheer mockery. To the gloom enveloping me I said aloud: "You never expected this."

Far from enjoying the rainy season that Sirhan al-Hilaly had predicted, I could not even think. Any idea I conceived came to nothing, shriveling as the wells of contemplation dried up. It was death, a living death: I saw death, touched it, smelled it, and lived with it.

When the money was all gone, I went to see Sirhan al-Hilaly at home. He didn't begrudge me an extra hundred pounds over and above the contracted price.

I'd entered a race with death, but I was so dried up within me that mine had become a living body without a soul. The voice of annihilation stole into my ears, jeering, letting me know that I was finished—it had played with me as it wished, baring its fangs to pronounce a sentence of death.

When the money ran out again, I rushed off a second time to Sirhan al-Hilaly, who politely but firmly made it clear that he was ready to grant me another sum whenever I showed him a portion of a new play—and only then.

Returning to solitude, with destitution now added to grief and sterility, I contemplated seeking a haven—Bab al-Shariya—but something stopped me. At that point, willfully parentless, soon to be homeless, and no longer belonging to any quarter, I said to myself that nothing was left except the end I'd assigned to my own protagonist. And eventually I hit upon the appropriate exit line. I despised my burdens and afflictions. No mention of them. I would die keeping them to myself.

Shortly before the call to afternoon prayers, I

went to the Japanese Garden* and sat down on a bench, oblivious of what was going on around me, aware only of my own thoughts in lurid collision with one another: *By what means? And when?*

I'd only slept an hour the night before. The wind blew, my head grew heavy, daylight was rapidly fading. Lassitude crept over me.

When I opened my eyes it was dusk, darkness falling with ponderous slowness; I must have slept for an hour or more. I got up from the bench—to find myself rising with unexpected buoyancy, filled with energy. My head was free of fever, my heart from its weight—how marvelous!—gloom had dispersed, depression had vanished, and I was a completely different person. *When had he been born? How had he been born? And why?* What had happened in the space of an hour?

I hadn't slept through an hour, but an era, from which I'd awakened into a new one. Something had happened during my sleep, something so preciously significant that surely, had it not been for this joy at sudden recovery, this joy that had loosened at last my death grip on memory and cast into oblivion even the recollection of priceless things, I might have been able to call to mind at least an inkling of the onset of this miraculous change. I could only think that somehow I must have com-

* A public garden at Helwan decorated with Japanese statues and laid out in Japanese style.

pleted a long and successful journey. From where otherwise—and how—had the resurrection come? Incomprehensible, unbidden, perhaps undeserved —but so tangible, so real that it could be seen and felt, in the very midst of spiritual emptiness and physical destitution, despite all opposition, obstacles, losses, and sorrows—this joy was all I wanted to cling to, this ecstasy, as if to a talisman. *Let its strength remain unfathomably in its mystery! Lo, its life-giving force marches forward, bearing with it the fragrance of triumph!*

I set out at once for the station, which was no mean distance away, and with every step new vigor rushed in, as full of promise as great clouds laden with rain—potentiality, feeling, responsiveness, far above and beyond the fact that I was penniless and pursued and carried sadness with me. Only after I'd covered a considerable stretch did I suddenly remember the note and realize that it was too late to retrieve it. I told myself that it didn't matter, that nothing mattered now—let whatever might happen to that letter happen, whatever the outcome might be—except to keep on going. *This ecstasy at its peak may glow on a body stripped by penury, bared to its own aridity, but on a will that the challenge of joy has made free.*

Book Mark

THE TEXT OF THIS BOOK WAS COMPOSED
IN FOURNIER BY CRANE TYPESETTING SERVICE,
WEST BARNSTABLE, MASSACHUSETTS

THE DISPLAY TYPE IS ABBOTT OLD STYLE AND LUCIAN
AND WAS COMPOSED BY ZIMMERING ZINN MADISON,
NEW YORK, NEW YORK

THE TEXT WAS PRINTED ON 50# HERITAGE BOOK ANTIQUE
AT R. R. DONNELLEY & SONS COMPANY,
CRAWFORDSVILLE, INDIANA

BOOK DESIGN BY BEVERLEY VAWTER GALLEGOS